Boundaries

Aiden Shaw has been a photographer and director of pop promos, a model and an actor. Whilst continuing his visual and performance art interests, he made a living as a prostitute and as a star in hardcore pornographic films in California. *Brutal*, his first novel was highly praised on publication in 1996; 'Aiden Shaw has until now been saluted as Britain's first hardcore porn film star,' Paul Smith wrote in *Gay Scotland*. 'However, with *Brutal* he also demonstrates his ability to write a powerful story. He has not so much stripped bare as stripped to the soul.' The *Lambda Book Report* commented that 'In a series of short, well-constructed, and simply written chapters the author displays quite a talent for pointed insight into the ways we communicate with friends, family and self.' *If Language at the Same Time Shapes and Distorts Our Ideas and Emotions, How Do We Communicate Love?*, a slim volume of poems, appeared in 1997, provoking Paul Burston to comment in *Time Out* that 'Aiden Shaw finally proves the pen is mightier then the penis' and *Mandate* to enthuse over 'A gusty accomplishment.' He is currently writing songs and performing with his band Whatever and completing a third novel.

Boundaries

Aiden Shaw

Millivres Books
Brighton

First Published in 1999 by Millivres Books (Publishers)
33 Bristol Gardens, Brighton BN2 5JR, East Sussex, England

Boundaries
Copyright © Aiden Shaw, 1999
The moral rights of the author have been asserted

A CIP catalogue record for this book is available from the British Library

ISBN 1 873741 48 0

Typeset by Hailsham Typesetting Services, 2 Marine Road,
Eastbourne, East Sussex BN22 7AU

Printed and bound by Biddles Ltd., Walnut Tree House, Woodbridge Park, Guildford, Surrey GU1 1DA

Distributed in the United Kingdom and Western Europe by Turnaround Distribution Ltd., Unit 3, Olympia Trading Estate, Coburg Road, Wood Green, London N22 6TZ

Distributed in Australia by Stilone Pty Ltd, PO Box 155, Broadway, NSW 2007, Australia.

Boundaries is
Dedicated to Flora, Joseph Holtzman, David Michael, Daniele Minns, Marcus Wayland
For being there when I really needed you.
I Love you.

Patrick Merla, Jess Wood, Sheila Roche, Julian Thomas, Dori, RonniLyn Pustil, Scott Link, Peter Burton, Sean Strub
For making this book happen

Steve Maguire, Gail Maguire, Danillo, Liz Fletcher, Caron, Ken Bunch, Rambo & Dean, Gareth Owen, Vicky Heller, Russell Martin, Paul Black, Leena Similu, Sam & Eamon, Rod Roderick, Andy Logan, Danny, Eli Whitney, Peter Armstrong, 'S', Paul Rutherford, Perry, Ray & Deba, Josie Jones, Annie, Ron Brock, Desmond Backhouse-Brady, Lucy Backhouse-Brady , Neil Kaczor, Kenny C, Jay Man O' Ray, Mathew Fisher, Jem Le Crem, Kali, Mick Bevan, Trish Stephenson, Trev, Dan, Richard Torie, Pierre et Gilles, Polly, James & James, Paul Burston, Michael Cullen, David Wolf, Edison, David Hodgson, Stuart Who?, Tony at *QX*, Andy Gashe, Paul Franckeiss, Yan Javeri, Andrew Harris, Lee Freeman, Lauren, Johan Insanally, Jeremy, George Fahouris, Jordi, Nick and Hussein, Joseph, Rob Cochrane, Gerard Floyd, Henrique, GGreg Debora Taylor, Suzi Kruger, Steven Scarborough, Craig Latker, Anthony Styant, Geoff Horsley, Donald, Phillip & Sue, Tom Allen, Scot Rafety, David Batty, Doctor Giles, Doctor Mike Yule, Ilan, Roma, Joel Von Ranson, John Derrybunce, B.J., Miss Kimberly, Richard Owen, Lawrence Schimel, George, Melanie Cassidy, Jim Reich, Lola Holah, Stella Stein, Polly, Ivan, The Divine David, Mark Anthony, Kinky Roland, Ran & Alcidez, Antoine, Fat Tony, Justin Shelley, Nina Minns, Paul Cooper, Douglas, Triksy Tracey, Cameron Laux, Wayne Shires, Kathleen, Gerard, Michelle, Christopher, Phillip & Simon, Tu Tu, Mathew Glamore, Johnny Flate, Dan Mc Cafferty, Richard, Jorge Quiroz, Mark Langey, Roland, Marc Almond, Joey Arias, Fat Tony, Mum, Dad, Lawrence Malice, Lee, Geoffrey Hinton, Michael Fenton,

David Porter, Walter Armstrong, Dean Chiarelli, Gene, Mark Duggan, Steady, Sexton Ming, Mark O' Flaherty, Link Leisure, Gearlyn, Peter & Josh, David Cabaret, Lee McQueen, David & Steve, Guido, Luke Warm, Baillie Walsh, Jonnie Shand Kydd, Joseph, Rifat, John Maybury, Alan McDonald, Rupert, Last, but sooooo not least, Princess Julia
For making life sweet and interesting

SENT

A blue-bottle buzzed loudly as it flew. Crossing a white wall, it landed. The bug set off again. Its wings rattled. Landing again, it decisively moved in all directions. A man turned his face to watch the twitching of its legs and wings. An obscure job done, the insect continued its mission.

A woman with a bottle of perfume in her hand pressed the atomizer. A soft mist released. Spray slid into the air surrounding the fly. The man collapsed into her lap. Putting her hand lovingly onto his face she said,

'"Sent." It's deadly.'

Silence.

'Perfect!' said Joe. 'And cut.'

The assistant director waved her pen in the air to get Joe's attention. 'Is that the take?' she asked.

'Oh yes,' said Joe.

'Okay, that's a wrap,' she shouted. 'I want the set down in half an hour, please!'

Joe whispered into her ear, then she continued, 'And will the actors please see Joe, before they leave. Thanks everybody.'

David changed, cleaned off his makeup and made his way to Joe's room. The other model had got there first. Waiting outside, David listened to the murmurs within. A girl came out, unrecognizable from earlier. Instead of her waist length folds of black hair and reptilian persona, now stood a fresh girl with short thin curls; insipid, but for a strong nose.

'Good news?' he asked.

Rolling her eyes, she yelped, 'No, nothing really. Just - if anything comes up. You know!'

'Are you going to the Coca-Cola casting?'

'No. Hunks only.' She overstated a smile and hitched her huge bag over her shoulder. 'Catch you later.' Humming a Pepsi jingle, she skipped off down the hall.

David knocked on the door. Not hearing a response, he did it again.

'I said come in. Ah! David?'

There was something familiar about Joe. It connected him to the character of the 'Sent' woman. Not that he looked like her. It was difficult to piece together. He seemed to stare.

'Is there anything wrong?' said David cheekily.

Joe was taken by surprise and instinctively retaliated. 'I would like to take you to dinner.'

As he spoke, he was conscious of his trembling leg hidden under the table.

'Dinner, no...Uhm, sorry...no.'

'Why not?' asked Joe, showing his vulnerability.

'I don't want to,' said David as he started to leave. 'I'm sorry.' He looked back at Joe and closed the door.

Stupid, stupid, stupid, Joe said to himself. He slammed his fist onto the table. His thumb nail cut into his finger. It seemed whatever way he chose to approach David, whatever Joe was, or could have been, wouldn't have got him what he wanted.

LOVE

It was rush-hour on the tube and most people were acting accordingly. Some read, others watched their reflections, or daydreamed. Flora skimmed through her newspaper.

Her eye caught a headline, 'Scarred inside and out.' This was the lead-in for an explicit description of an attack. The story had been given particularly good coverage because it was about a man who'd been raped. Flora rested the paper on her lap. She thought for a moment, then pulled out a pad from her briefcase and wrote, 'Death is more interesting than life. Devastation is more interesting than growth. Suffering is more interesting than bliss.'

Out of the corner of her eye, Flora noticed some commotion. The tube door had opened and tried to close, but something was obstructing it. Flora checked her watch, then looked round. She saw someone lying in the doorway, their head and arm on the platform.

'Hold the door,' she shouted, with no trace of alarm, only surprise that no one had done this already. 'You, hold the door,' Flora said, to a woman, who wanted only to recoil, not get involved. The attention she might receive, if she refused, seemed unbearable, so she did as she was told. Arching over the man on the floor she managed, by becoming a wedge, to stop the doors closing. This typing, tea-making, sandwich-fetching woman surprised herself. Already someone else had come to help, a girl in a school uniform. These two looked at each other. At this moment they understood something that words could only clumsily have communicated.

'Does anyone have a mobile phone?' asked Flora; then looking round, '...quickly... a mobile phone.' Someone did. It was rush hour, so the tube was full of useful people. 'Call an ambulance...Is there a doctor here?' Then at the top of her voice, 'Is there a doctor on this train?'

A timid young girl nudged her way through the watching people.

'I'm a nurse,' came her quiet voice.

'Great.'

This only-just-left-her-teens girl, knelt beside the man. A group of boys came to help. The girl directed them. 'Let's get him on to the platform. Be careful,' she said.

Flora asked the girl if she had time to stay with the man.

'I think they'll understand at the hospital,' she said with a cheeky smile. Getting back on the tube Flora thanked the women who held the door. A guardsman, with a cup of tea in his hand, got the doors closed and the train moved off.

Finally home, as though automated, Flora took off her scarf, undressed out of her crisp, tailored, smartness, and simultaneously dressed into comfortably constructed casualness. This was different to her normal routine. She carried something inside, and it waited. As she clicked on the cooker, it waited. As she set the whole kitchen in action, it still waited. Then it hovered, as she approached her desk, as she opened her computer. A coil released. Letters flicked onto the screen, spelling out thoughts. Words, fluid with control, were rhythmically placed, amidst stops, then bolts of passion:

I have love. It is not the regimented kind, contrived by romantics. It is not that which came before, which focused on the rearing of young and, perhaps, even some pleasant company.

The one I know is very modern. It is about accepting every part of someone, each fault, the shit, the scum, the filth and the hate of them. Loving these, because it's them, in the same way that these are a part of you and must be loved.

This more modern love is an eternal love. It can't be quantified. It is all, like a love for a God, or from a child, but more than both. Unlike a God, it is truly reciprocated, and unlike a child, there is a choice. Within this love there are highlights and dullish times, which can last seconds or much longer. However the dynamics of this love change, it is still the same thing. Almost anyone is capable of this, but not all find it. Many get something, like in other areas of their life, which only suffices.

Like your soul, this love must be discovered. It's not so simple to find. There is no short cut, no cheating it out of anyone, or yourself. Watch within yourself and know something special in life, know you. When you do, how you look at other people will change forever.

I look at everyone around me and see that they all shine from within. Deep inside, they have a tenderness which must never be shat on. When you have this love, no one can take from you, it is you.

Flora rubbed her hair, put her hands under her chin and smiled. The front door buzzer sounded. She answered it, then quickly returned to her computer, closed the file labeled "You," headed towards the kitchen and got busy with the dinner.

AFFIRMATIONS

'Carbine Lane, Docklands please.'

'Right it is...Off we go,' said the cabby whilst checking out his fare in the rearview mirror. David looked to one side. Aware the driver was watching, he looked to his other side and out of the window. The pavement slid by, attracting only part of David's attention.

'Shouldn't you be watching the road,' said David, coolly, without facing the eyes, the stubble, the sexy, sexual stare.

'Yeah, guess so, but I know these streets like my wife... you know, don't need to look any more.'

'I see.'

'Get my gist?'

'I hear you.'

'You married, mate?'

'No, well...maybe.'

'What do you mean maybe, you are or you're not.'

'Well, it depends how you look at it. I'm committed to someone, but technically we're not married.'

'Ah, I get you. Best way, then you can dump 'em when you're done... no financial strings... yeah very nice.'

'No, it's not like that. I wouldn't want to dump them...' Flora came to mind, his feelings shifted to confusion. Instantly, another idea took its place. He decided to tease the driver. 'We can't get married, we're both men.'

A greedy smile slashed its way across the driver's face. Framed, and rectangle, it floated like the Cheshire Cat's. His eyes bobbed up and down, finally catching David's. Neither looked away.

'They have a club you know.'

'Who?'

'The gays. Yeah, they meet up most nights. There's lots of them, you know.'

'I know.'

'How long you known then?'

'About the club?'

'No, that you were a... gay.'

'Always, I guess. But the first time I did it, that was

when I was sure.'
  'Did what?'
  'You know.'
  'No,' the driver answered. Yet he seemed to be asking a question at the same time. He tried to lure David with a calculated naivete. 'No, what is it they do?'
  'Just here please, beside the blue door. Thanks. How much is that?'
  'Oh yeah... err... that it'll be...four pounds.'
  'Thanks very much.'
  'Nice place to live,' says the driver.
  'Yeah...' Then, within the edge of the same second, '...I bet it would be.'
  David closed the cab door, paid, checked the road for traffic, then crossed to his apartment. He fumbled in his pockets for keys, hoping to kill time until the cab left. The driver appeared to be reading a newspaper, in no hurry to go anywhere. David thought to press the buzzer, nonchalantly looking back, before he closed the door.
  There was nothing interesting in the mail box, just junk, which David sifted through as he walked over to the lift. A man was standing there, already waiting. They looked at each other. He wore overalls and was carrying a tool box. The lift arrived. The man followed David, but maneuvered in behind him, to his side. David wanted to take a look, but something told him not to. At the same time, his forehead dragged his face around just enough to realise that he was being looked at. This scared David and he wasn't sure if it was the man, or something in himself that was the cause. It was enough of a signal for David to turn a little more. And in long seconds this continued. It might have ended with a smack, a sneer, a laugh, or perhaps a smile, a wink, or a breath of passion. He turned some more, even more towards the stranger, who had been watching all this time. David wanted to speak. He wanted to be American, say something stupid, something used, friendly and intrusive. Nothing came out, only voiceless, fearful lies.
  'Are they Nike?' the man said, towards David's feet.
  'Yeah, they're my second pair.'

'They're hiking boots aren't they?'

'I don't know,' said David, bringing their talk to an end.

The lift stopped. The stranger got out feeling disappointed. After all, 'Are they Nike?' wasn't the question he'd meant to ask, 'Can I kiss you?' was.

BEYOND WORDS

'Forgot your keys?'
'No.'
'Why did you ring the buzzer?'
'Oh, nothing, I'm just being paranoid.'
'Something bothering my Lambsy?'
'Not really, just some creepy cabby.'
'Arh baby, no need to be scared. Flora's here now.'

David dropped his bag beside her desk and followed her into the kitchen.

'How was your shoot?'
'Slick, chic...slightly twisted.'
'Let me guess, a car ad. No. Perfume!'
He laughed. 'Are they that predictable?'
'Hey... It sells.'
'I know....and it pays.'
'Yes, more importantly.'

David started to serve dinner as Flora prepared a salad. The food was unappetizing, but very nutritious.

'What shall I pretend this tastes like today?' said David chasing one of his shelled egg whites with a fork.

'Shut up and eat up.'

'Yes, Ma'am.' David was quiet for a moment whilst he cut, forked, chewed and swallowed. 'My God you won't believe what happened after the shoot.'

'What?'

'The director called me to his office and, get this, he tried to pick me up.'

'You're joking?'

'Honest to God. He asked me out for dinner.'

'Barking up the wrong tree, poor thing. What did you say?' Flora couldn't help grinning.

'I said no of course. What should I have said, "Yes, and maybe, you could come back to my place afterwards for coffee."'

'And?'

'"And meet my girlfriend Flora-pain-in-the-neck."'

'You could have schmuzled some work out of the queen.'

'He's no queen.'
'You sound defensive.'
'Yeah right. No, I would never have guessed if he weren't so open. I kind of liked him'
'Oh. Watch out.'
'God you're tiring. It's a good job I love you.'
'Or?'
'Or, I might run off with Joe.'
'Oh, so, it's Joe now is it.'
'Yes. Joe and I can't get enough of each other you know.'

They laughed at their conversation and spent the rest of their meal talking about things they had done whilst apart. As they cleared the dishes, the front door buzzer sounded. Flora headed out of the kitchen, 'I'll get it.'

After a moment David shouted, 'Who is it?' His curiosity got the better of him. Drying his hands, he headed towards the living room, repeating, 'Who is it?'

A man's voice replied, 'It's me, Joe.'
'Ah...Joe.' David was shocked, yet not surprised. Flora seemed amused. 'How did you know where I lived?'
'The A.D. had your address. I hope you don't mind.'
'Why should I mind? Confused maybe. Did I leave something?'
'No, not that I know of.'
'Did you have something to tell me?'
'No.'

At this point Flora burst out laughing, 'I'm sorry. I don't mean to... really I'm sorry.' She tried to ease the situation, more for herself than for David. 'Are you thirsty? Can I get you anything?'

'I'd love some tea,' said Joe, disarming her with a warm smile.
'A cup of tea it is.'
'David, anything for you?'
'Yeah, tea's fine.'

As she left the room, Flora carried on talking, so as not to leave them completely alone.
'So you're a director. That must be interesting.'

Joe had entered into a conversation of looks with David.

After a pause, he said to Flora, 'Yes, sometimes.' He spoke loudly, so he could be heard from the kitchen. His eyes did not break from David's the whole time. There was another pause. Flora heard the silence, but not their communication.

'Why only sometimes?' she continued, a little labored.

'It's like anything, there's lots of rubbish involved.'

Again a resounding quiet. The two men continued to communicate.

What are you doing here?
I don't know.
What do you want?
You, I think.

Joe broke this dialogue with words.

'Is there anything wrong?'

'I don't know,' said David.

'Do you want me to leave?'

'No,' said Flora, as she re-entered the room. 'Have some tea, it's made now.'

Flora and David were working on a relationship; "working," because it didn't just happen. Like many people they found comfort in each other's company. They felt lust and were kind to each other. They, like many, believed that their partner made them a better person, more what they wanted to be. So they decided to try and make this "better them" a permanent thing. Neither of them ever again wanted to find themselves what they were before, whether lonely and cruel or desperate and selfish. They had a lot to avoid by joining together.

Go away, said the voice in David's head. Yet he also whispered, *You could be my father or my brother.* Beyond the conscious, there was a trickle of protection and strength, hidden from his conditioning and sex.

Fuck off Joe, get out of here. No. No don't!

David wanted to be treated with kisses that didn't ask him to perform. The kind a father sends to his child, each time he holds, he touches, he whispers into its soul.

'Who wants to cut the air?' said Flora, holding up a knife.

They all laughed. Hesitantly at first. Then it built and continued. Something was released. Something bonded. They knew each other at least a little now. They had shared a laugh.

INSIDE

I turn the light off and close my eyes. I open them again, but quickly close them. Lying with my eyes open, thinking, isn't something I do now. Not what I do at bedtime since way back.

I open my eyes. What's the point of looking into the darkness? All I can see are shapes of objects and tones of paintwork. I know the point: life can be nothing, can go by smoothly and hardly noticed. Or, it can be heightened; altering and moving. Life can be noticeable, by looking into the dark, when I am meant to be trying to fall asleep. I know if I'm not careful, if I don't get in the right position, or if I leave it too long, everything will be ruined and I'll probably have to get up and go to the toilet and possibly even eat. Then I'll have to brush my teeth, to avoid ulcers in my mouth. By opening my eyes and looking around my room, I am going against the rules I've created to help me fall asleep. But look how pretty the barely half-light is, coming from behind the blind. Look how sculptured from nothingness everything has become, all partially not there, yet gesturing their presence as well. Perfect things, perfect room, perfect peace, by simply opening my eyes and ignoring my rules.

I close my eyes. I must go to sleep. Occasionally, I take a tablet. That's if I need a good night's rest. If I have something important to do the next day. Something more important than feeling a heightened, altering, moving, noticeable and glorious presence, there behind my lids - outside, in my room.

I do have to go to the toilet. I switch on the glow of the night light, the orange glow of the ... I can feel it, I can feel...that life can be heightened, etc. So I live another few seconds and this life seems strong and pathetic, very felt and noticeable. I go to the bathroom and on my return I'm confronted, as I'm always confronted, by myself, through my room. I stand on my concrete floor. And I want to be things: good, clever, tuned in, reaching my limits. So I turn the dimmer on the switch, now a little more, and I bring on feeling after feeling, a blur of response. Thinking and smelling, and noticing detail, I remember that I must turn the light off. If I don't, my room will keep me alert all night.

I slide over the floor in my socks and sit on the edge of my bed. I laugh at the silly skater in me. Quietly, I say "Thank you." I say it to my room, my desk, my shoes and door.

I think to myself, "Now, you must go to bed. You must go to sleep." Also, "Be kind. Please be kind to yourself, because so few will." I pick up a small bottle of lavender oil, from my window sill. I put a few drops on my pillow. "Goodnight, I love you," are my final spoken thoughts. I pull up my blanket, close to my chin and snuggle down. I feel so loved by my bedroom.

BEYOND ACTION

At the heart of a large house, within a sparse room, sat a man. He was lit by a small angle lamp. His concentration was complete. The comforts around him, may as well have not existed. This was something he had learnt to do, out of necessity. Without light, without kindness, he had managed to grow, like a weed through layers of concrete. Weed. With such a name, how could anyone appreciate it. Nature didn't give this name. Weed is a word we have created for something that happens to be where we don't want it, an inconvenience, a nuisance. This was Joe, or rather something he had been. After all, it was only a perception.

With a pair of tweezers, Joe picked up a dead wasp. He applied a tiny bob of glue to its abdomen, then placed it on a vase, which was already half covered. The telephone rang.

'Flora... yeah me too...great yeah...I'd love you to...right. Eight o'clock sharp.'

Joe was having an art exhibition. Flora and David confirmed that they'd go to the opening. The event instantly had more meaning for Joe. He clapped his hands, as if to wake up, or bring himself back to another reality. This seemed like a different man to the one only minutes before. After checking the time, he calculated the rest of his day. Then, he resumed his work and the moodless persona of before.

When finishing his work, Joe left everything as it was. There was no need to tidy anything away. No one would see the mess. He had no visitors. None were ever invited.

Joe dressed with special care, enjoying the ceremony of his work. The exhibition was prestigious. A one-man show at the Institute of Contemporary Art. He hoped it would be painless.

David and Flora arrived together, looking lovely, individually, and as a couple. They offered refuge, so Joe willingly took it. Like the walls of his home, his new friends protected him from other people.

'So what do I think?' said Flora.

Joe feigned a wince. 'I wasn't going to ask, but now that you have.'

'I'm not going to comment yet, I haven't seen enough.'

'Don't expect me to answer any questions,' said Joe.

'That's fine by me,' said David.

'And me,' said Flora, who led the way, through the crowd. David brought up the rear. They stopped in front of an exhibit. Secretly, Joe hoped to understand Flora and David, by how they responded to his work.

'What is it? A book?' said David.

Joe nodded and without saying a word, he pointed to the title, "The Things I Fear The Most About Myself."

'Did you write it?'

'It's a sculpture,' said Joe.

'Oh,' said David, thinking he was on his way to understanding it.

'Sorry. Yes. I wrote it.'

Flora smiled and nodded her head.

'Has it been published?' she asked.

'No.'

'How can people read it then?' she continued.

'One at a time.'

'Can I read it?' asked Flora.

Joe smiled. 'I'd love you to.'

Flora swayed with flirtation. Both men noticed.

With this book, Joe had wanted to excavate himself. This wasn't about aesthetics. It was about trying to discover truths. The plan was to find, within himself, the place of all his scum and bathe there for a while. The book was an expression of what he found.

The mixed media exhibits didn't say anything specifically, but made the whole room feel as though something importantly wrong had been done. Flora understood something of this. David was confused, but affected by the work.

A car waited outside, and after only an hour and a half, they left. Once back at Flora and David's, all three finally relaxed. It was already clear that they felt good in each other's company. Flora rolled a joint, David heated some milk and Joe chose a C.D. They began to mellow.

'It's all about money you know...' Joe couldn't be bothered to continue. 'Blah, blah, blah,' is all he could muster.

'Blah, blah, blah, what?' said David.

'It's all bullshit,' said Joe.

'What?'

'All of it.'

'Don't you like being an artist?'

'No. Yes. Well, I like creating, but that's not the same thing.'

'Explain,' demanded Flora, joining the conversation.

'Okay. You asked for it.'

'Go on,' said Flora licking the paper of another joint, and meticulously sticking it together.

'Well, you can buy art, right?'

'Right,' said David.

'But you can't buy creativity.'

'So what are they buying?' David was pleased to be keeping up with the discussion.

'Here comes the cynical bit. I think they're buying money.'

'What do you mean?' said Flora. She enjoyed the way Joe thought.

'Once art has a value, it becomes currency.'

'Well put,' said Flora.

'Clever, clever,' said David.

'Now, you're embarrassing me.'

'Yeah, sure. It would take a lot more than that to embarrass you,' said David and scuffed Joe's hair. Joe blushed.

'But why not buy gold bars,' said Flora.

Joe's speech slowed down. He thought as he spoke. 'Maybe, these people have no creativity in their lives. So they try and buy it.' He laughed at himself. 'All they really get is an image of it, a facsimile.'

'I suppose this is enough for most people,' said Flora. 'Superficially, it's decorative.'

'Yeah. It seems to work.' Joe resigned a smile. 'Don't get me wrong. I think creativity is magical.'

'Hear! Hear!' said Flora.

'Yeah! Like what you said,' added David. Using his best Californians accent.

All three burst out laughing. They were getting stoned. Joe stretched in front of the fire. Turning over, he let his weight squash his crotch. One side of his face warmed and went pink. Watching his friends, he laughed at their jokes and made some of his own. It was as though his blood, having its own life, was tickling his insides, stomach and balls. David caught Joe looking, a breath too long, both looked away. As though it had significance, their eyes turned to Flora.

'This fire is gorgeous, but I'm burning up,' said Joe, hoping to distract his company.

'You know my baby sings,' said Flora.

'Don't you?' said Joe.

'Not like David. You should hear him.'

'I'd love to, sometime.'

'Baby,' said Flora, 'Why don't you do it now?'

David looked at Joe. 'Do you want me to?'

'Only if you're comfortable.'

'Sure, it's no big deal,' said David.

'You're being modest. We'll see afterwards if Joe thinks it's no big deal.'

David looked uncomfortable. After a slight pause, something happened, which was probably complex, but it seemed to come easily to David. Opening his mouth, without changing his expression, came notes. They slipped out with ease, mutating one to another. Joe's listened in silence. David stopped and hung his head.

'Is there anything wrong?' said Flora, looking at Joe.

'No. That was beautiful, really beautiful.'

Joe felt himself recoiling. Humiliated in being opened so much. He cooled, becoming cold within seconds. The amount of time it takes to feel stupid, become insecure and feel alone. In a room of such warmth, he cut himself off. Luckily, it was understood differently.

'Are you tired?' said Flora.
'I think so.'
'Why don't you stay here. We have a spare room.'

Thinking it backed up his lie, Joe found himself accepting. It felt as though there was no way out. Maybe he wanted nothing more than to sleep close to Flora and David. This is what they wanted. It made them feel good, when they went to bed, knowing he was in the room next door. When they made love and pigged out, they were quiet, so as not to disturb Joe. They both fantasized about fucking with him. Neither told the other.

Meanwhile, Joe felt a little weird. He stared ahead, with his fingers crossed over his tummy. There was a picture at the end of his bed. In it, a little boy sat cross-legged on some fluorescent green grass. Beside the boy was a duckling. Looming over them both was a dog with a hard-on. Hung around the dog's neck was an identity collar. It read David. The child's face expressed a mix of fear and pleasure. Behind the figures, a tornado sucks up everything in its path. A trail of damage is left. The colors reminded Joe of a dress his mother once wore. He fell into a reverie of lemonade, screeching children and orangey-red lipstick, so elegant and sure. He's holding the lipstick in his girly-boy fingers. Sitting in front of a mirror, he's trying to create in himself everything that his mother was to him. 'Snowy-Joey,' was being called by some children. Then this was replaced by the drone of a teacher's voice. Joe was falling asleep now. He could see himself, his bleached looking skin and beige/blonde hair, his standing alone whilst others played around him. Now David was standing over him, both were adults. Lifting his foot David pushed it against Joe's lips. One by one David's toes slipped into his mouth. Joe could smell sweat, washing powder, and a hint of leather. David knelt down, his balls lowered. The shaft of his dick slid heavily over Joe's eyes and nose. Joe breathed, immersed in crotch. He felt doped up on musk.

Asleep and woman-like, Joe was now Flora. He massaged his clitoris and writhed around his bed. He wrapped his top sheet around his legs. Rolling it into a solid twist, he pulled it up between his thighs and lodged it firmly under his cunt. Breathing deeply, Joe took these smells into his gut. There they began to push around, manipulate the wall of his tummy.

Falling forward, David rested on his hands. Then crouching, he scuttled his feet down either side of Joe's body. Hovering over him, face to face, he pushed his chin deep into Joe's neck and kissed behind his ear. David lowered his torso, Joe began to feel the weight and shape of David's dick on his abdomen. As though doing press ups, David rose up and down. The head of his dick thumped against Joe. Each time David lifted, a sticky thread stretched, cooled, then fell away. Nestling down, he sighed as the shaft of his dick settled on to Joe's cunt. David rocked from side to side, using his hard dick as a pivot, all the time oozing precum. Joe could smell David's breath. It made him want to open, let David inside. 'Come in,' he said, as he groaned and came. Joe looked up and realised he'd been fucked by a dog. Feeling content Joe continued to sleep.

SHIT

Morning sunlight, shone through a stained-glass window on the landing. Joe woke-up and headed for the bathroom. As he stepped out of the guest bedroom, his face moved into green light. He looked down at his feet. A pool of red shone on the floor, beneath him. It crawled up his body, as he moved forward. A figure moved ahead of him. All Joe could see was the silhouette of a person, hallowed.

'Sorry, I didn't mean to...' said Flora, seeing that he wasn't quite dressed.

'Oh, Flora. No, I'm sorry.'

Not fully awake and susceptible, he saw the outline of her body. He noticed the light through her dress. A prod from his groin flicked his balls. This clenched his dick, still swollen from sleep. He had the urge to hold her, and to coat her skin, as the light did. If only he could be that close. Even, be in her mouth when she spoke.

'I'm just...the bathroom,' she said.

'Yes, right. Uhm, me too.'

'Oh sorry, go ahead.'

'No-no. No, it's yours...I mean it's all yours.'

Flora noticed Joe's stare. It surprised her. She liked it. At this point, they both realised there was something sexual between them. Joe smiled. Flora felt a rush in her cunt.

'I'll see you downstairs,' he said. They both pulled smiles.

'Yes.'

A few moments later, Flora and Joe both sat in the kitchen waiting for David. There was a plain-wrapped parcel, on the counter top.

'The bomb was supposed to arrive after I'd left,' Joe said. Flora responded with a wimpy laugh.

'Scrambled eggs okay?' she said. Joe nodded. 'Would you like anything in them? Mushrooms, tomatoes?'

'Both would be great.' Flora turned back toward the cooker. Joe checked out the room, whilst not being watched. 'I slept well.'

'That bed's just like ours. They're so comfortable.' This

wasn't what he meant. It was because he felt good that he'd slept well. His attention fell on the parcel. Flora caught him looking at it.

'Isn't someone going to open that,' he said.

'Why don't you open it?' said Flora.

'It's not addressed to me.'

'You're not David?'

'No, sorry.'

David walked into the room.

'Moaning.'

'Moaning yourself.'

'Sorry.'

Joe smiled. It had been a long time since he had played like this.

'What's this?' said David, looking at the parcel.

'How should we know?' said Flora.

'I meant who's it for?' He picked it up and read who it was addressed to. 'It's for me, of course.' The parcel was difficult to open, so David got a small kitchen knife to cut the tape. Just as he was finishing, the knife slipped and dug inside the box. 'Oops, I hope it isn't alive.'

'Wasn't alive,' said Joe.

David opened the box and saw a shiny surface. He put both hands in, expecting glass or plastic, something fragile. 'Its soft,' he said, grinning. Then, as he lifted the object out, he noticed that it was dripping. He suddenly became aware of what it was and dropped it onto the counter. 'Ugh! It's shit! Jesus Christ! It's a bag of shit.'

Joe led David by the arm, to the sink. He turned on the hot water, tested it, then put David's hands underneath. Opening the cupboard beneath the sink, Joe found disinfectant and poured it over David's hands. Checking three drawers in succession, Joe found bin bags. He ripped one off, and put the bag and the box inside. The whole of the mess was wiped away before David turned back around. Joe looked at Flora who, until now, had stood watching. With an expression and a flick of his head, he gestured for Flora to help, to comfort David. She did. David accepted. It was impossible not to love him in this state. Joe and Flora both treated him tenderly until he seemed more calm and present. They all sat in silence. Nobody felt like eating breakfast.

SADO MASOCHISM

Some things always seem to happen at night. People live their daily lives which sometimes, often, differ from their nightly lives. This may be out of practicality, concerning the conscience, which doesn't like to be seen by the day. It's a little like not wanting to have sex with the light on, only less about the body and more about the mind. Souls come together to explore their dark sides, their usually hidden-away sides. This is the realm of fear and trust. Master and Recipient. There is no play-acting here.

A fluorescent strip lights this space, a dungeon or playroom. There are contraptions here that have been created especially by the Master. One of them is a slightly cushioned table, onto which a figure is strapped. In the center of this table is a pivot, so that the whole thing can turn three hundred and sixty degrees. This means a person could lie with their face up and turn right over so the whole of their body weight hangs face down. The sensation can be anything from an exciting ride at a funfair to being securely held like a baby.

The man in this contraption has a lattice work of leather straps, with over forty buckles crossing his body, keeping him in place. Through the squares and rectangles, his flesh is naked and hairless, his body having been shaved in preparation.

Removing your clothes can make you feel vulnerable enough. Add to this a blindfold. Then, the knowledge that you are going to be shaved from neck to foot with a straight blade. You have been told to keep still, so you do. Very still. Even when the blade maneuvers around your nipples, then your arse and balls. Imagine what goes through your head as the sack of your scrotum is lifted up, and gently pulled, so that all the hairs can be reached.

Over this landscape of black leather straps, pits of skin and highlights of metal, something protrudes. Sectioned off, in an area of its own, a dick and balls splendidly sit. A focus point perhaps, but there are other ways to think. And other things to experience before the deadening event of an orgasm.

The table is turned three times. Slowly, so that the blood can adjust. A strap covers the eyes, but the mouth is left free. This Master could hear how anxious or exhilarated the recipient feels. On the last turn, the table is left at an angle, leaning forward, just past the vertical. The body neither rests on the cushion nor on the straps, but sits comfortably between the two.

'I'm going to put a mild acid on your skin. It won't harm you. Do you want me to do this?'

'Yes.'

There is no room here for indecision. No questions are allowed. 'What kind of acid? What strength?' or, 'Are you sure it won't harm me?' There is only one answer. It must be said with a confidence that shows you believe in your Master.

It may be clear, how wonderful this can be for the Master. How far will someone let you take them? How much belief and even love do they show for you during this process?

'Are you ready?'

'Yes.'

No indication is given where the acid will be poured. Would it be on his sensitive nipples, or worse, his face? The fluid is squirted from a plastic bottle, spraying lightly over the crotch. There is a loud scream. Through this, a voice is heard.

'Tell me how it feels.'

'It burns.'

'Do you trust me?'

'Yes.'

Invisible to the naked eye, a stirring takes place deep in a gut. Not like an erection or a cramping. More like the place where the physical sex of a person links with their thoughts, not their emotions.

Blowing gently over the crotch, the burning slowly stops.

'It's only alcohol, there's no need to worry. Unless this flame...' The recipient hears a lighter being lit, '...comes too close.' The Master lights a long thin piece of wood and passes it over a sweaty chest, singeing the odd stray hair, leaving fine wisps of smoke.

'Do you trust me?'

'Yes.'

If you could enter the thoughts of a submissive, at this time, you would be aware of sounds. The creak of leather and your own stammered breath. You would be acutely conscious of your Master's movements; the turning of gritty souls, footsteps walking away, stopping, then returning. Guessing at actions and possible consequences. All the time, reassuring yourself and trying to relax. It's only when you give in, when you abandon yourself completely; it's only then that barriers can be crossed.

You feel heat on your neck, around your chin, over your lips. You needn't flinch, your Master knows the right distance. Then, there is complete silence. So you listen. And because there seems to be nothing, you stifle your breath and you listen extra hard. At this point, you hear something you now recognize. The sound of the alcohol being picked up again. Your mind races forward. You forget to control yourself by trusting your Master and you say, 'Stop!' and you fail. You know in an instant that you're pathetic, that you don't deserve to belong to anybody. Especially, to someone who's careful and so meticulous in meeting your needs. You know that your Master knows your fears, that fire is one of your deepest; and yet, you fail. So lost in all your other fears, you fail.

When these thoughts subside you begin to think about the blindfold. Your focus is so small. It's on that one strap of leather. You obsess, because you know when the blindfold is removed, you've got to face your Master. Such shame. You've failed. There is no other way of looking at it. When you leave you replay time and time again. Rewinding, then dissecting every single moment. When you were strong. When you were good. When you still had some self-respect. That was before you gave in and became nothing in your mind. Would you even be allowed to try again?

DIS-EASE

All day, shit had been on all their minds. How could it not be? David had tried to find an explanation. Maybe it was rotten food; something perfectly harmless, like old birthday cake. The postal system was slow.

The smell was unmistakable. Everyone knows what shit smells like. It's even possible to differentiate kinds of shit, like cow, or bird, or in this case, possibly, human. It smelt less wholesome than cow's shit, more bitter than bird's. No, it was clear what it was, but less so, whose it was?

At some point during the day, an arrangement for dinner was made. Flora couldn't make it. She had a previous appointment with her ex-husband, which she had predictably forgotten. Even though they had been married for eight years, it was difficult for them to make lunch, or even coffee. They had no children to bind them, so barely kept in touch. He had found a woman who he said was great "in the sack." Flora felt this was a put-down, as though she wasn't.

Whilst married, Flora's husband slept with other women and she wanked. They both let this go on for quite some time, until her husband spent more time in other beds than in theirs. Eventually, they stopped pretending there was anything worth saving and split.

Joe suggested a quiet restaurant for dinner, which suited David fine. Although, he half expected a more fashionable place.

'Cute place,' said David facetiously.

'Don't you like it?'

'Yeah...' then as if suddenly agreeing with himself, 'It is cosy isn't it?'

'I like it,' said Joe.

Then, feigning intrigue and surprise, David said, 'There aren't any women here.'

'I noticed that too.'

'How strange.'

'It must be some kind of stag night,' said Joe.

'Right, that'll be it.'

David began to look worried.

'I can't stop thinking about it,' said Joe, preempting David's concerns.

'Me neither. Do you think it was,' he lowered his voice, 'shit?'

For a dreaded second, Joe thought David might call it "faeces" or, worse still, "stool." Even though David felt the need to lower his voice, Joe was relieved to hear the word "shit."

'I think it was. Do you have any idea who sent it?'

'I've been racking my brain all day,' said David.

'It's almost a shame that I threw the parcel away. There may have been some clues.'

'We didn't have much choice.'

'If only,' said Joe

'What?' said David.

'I was going to say, if only it had been recorded delivery.'

'Duh!'

'I know, I did stop myself.'

'Not quick enough.'

'Okay, okay.'

Joe's flawless pores folded in on each other, as he scrunched his face.

'What?' said David responding to his expression.

'We could fish it out of the bin. Check the postmark at least.'

'Ugh I couldn't. Really, I'd be sick.'

'I could do it.'

'But you wouldn't want to.'

'Of course not, but it might help.'

'That's very gallant of you. But, I'd rather you didn't.'

'Phew!'

David laughed, opening a space for Joe to change the topic of their conversation.

'Not to be too selfish, but it was a horrible end to my stay. I'd had such a nice evening.' Then, remembering how he'd felt as he went to bed, he nearly dwelt on this, but let it drop. 'It was sweet of you to let me stay.'

'Oh, it's nothing.'

'I know. But it's a nice gesture, don't you think?'

'I guess so.' David put his head down and adjusted his napkin. Joe could have patted the head of such cuteness, or simply fucked him until he said 'I love you.' On looking up, David caught him grinning.

'What's up with you?'

'Nothing, just you.'

'What do you mean?'

'You're so God damned sweet,' said Joe wistfully. 'Your mamma brought you up well... and you're not fooling anyone. Blushing is a dead giveaway.'

Caught out again, David threw his napkin at Joe and they giggled. 'Oh, I meant to ask you about the picture in my room. I mean, you know, the tornado one.'

'Aren't you forgetting the hard-on.'

'How could I?'

'Do you like it?' said David.

'The hard-on?'

'The picture.'

I don't know. Who made it?'

'Tell me first what you thought?'

'I like it.'

'Flora did it.'

'What's it about?'

'It's meant to be about me.'

'How's it about you?'

Here, David ground to a halt. 'Uhm.'

'You can't stop now, I won't let you.'

'Well, I don't want you to get the wrong impression.'

'I'll try not. Give me the dirt.'

'There is no dirt. It's just that...'

'Come on.'

'Flora always jokes about this boy...saying that I want to have sex with him.'

Joe raised his eyebrows. 'My God! She thinks you're a homosexual?'

'He's only seven. He's my nephew.'

Now Joe really was surprised. 'And do you?'

'No.'

'So she just made it all up?'
'No.'
'Well?'
'Promise you won't repeat this.'
'Of course.'
'It's just that he sat on my knee and I got a hard on.'
'Big deal.'
'Right, big deal.'
'So what.'
'Really, that's what I said.'
'Well, anyway, now Flora won't let it go. So she made that picture. The little boy is Ryan - that's his name. But, he's also me.'
'And?'
'Well, the duckling represents my vulnerability and the tornado my rage.'
'And the dog?'
'That's the beast in me.'
'The beast?'
'Flora explains it better.'
'I must talk to her about it. Does she have any others?'
'Uhm...yeah.'
David reached across the table and put his hand on Joe's

'I hope you don't think I'm weird. You know, about my nephew. I can't explain it very well. I do love him.'
'I understand.'
'You do?'
'Well, I haven't known you very long, but I understand that you wouldn't harm anyone. Would you?'
'Of course not. Not intentionally.'
'Right.'
'If he were an adult I would like sex with him.' David's openness was unnerving. '...but he's not.'

Their waiter arrived. 'Hello. Just water for me. David? A large bottle of water? Sparkling okay? Great.' Joe noticed David looking at the waiter's arse as he walked away.
'I understand,' said Joe, 'about your nephew.'

'Do you think it's creepy?'
'No.'
'I like you Joe.'
'About time.'
'I guess it's a good way of testing you.'
'Oh, so have I passed?'
'I'm afraid so.'

Joe pretended to cough. 'I like you too,' he said, but it was muffled by his hand.

'Sorry I didn't catch that?'

'I like you,' said Joe. This time it was loud enough for the whole restaurant to hear.

'I heard you the first time, sucker.'

Never before had Joe met anyone quite like David: naive, not stupid. Simple, but layered.

'What are you thinking?' David quizzed warily.

'All sorts of things.'

'You'll make me paranoid.'

'Oh, you've nothing to worry about.' Joe almost hoped David understood, but didn't want to spell it out. Not yet. 'Listen, I've had an idea. Why don't we go for a day out, to cheer you up. Help you forget about all this parcel stuff.'

'Where?'

'Somewhere. On my bike.'

'Uhm.'

'You don't have to do a thing, just sit pretty. You know how to do that.'

'Where would we go?'

'I don't know. I'll surprise you. I'll take care of you and I'll have you home before dark.'

'What about Flora?'

'She can live without you for a day.'

'No, I mean, maybe she'll want to come.'

'I've only got room for one.'

'Oh yeah. When were you thinking of?'

'Whenever, I'll work round you.'

'Okay. I'll just check with Flora. I'll call you tomorrow.'

'Great.'

OPEN HEART

'Who are these children?' asked David looking at a school photograph. 'Are they Judy's?'

'Yes, Ryan and Lynda. I can't believe you've never met them,' replied his brother, Ben. This wasn't so strange, as David hadn't seen any of his family for years. There were no Christmas, or anniversary get-togethers. Mother was dead and father was despondent. This could have been the cause.

David wondered how Judy and her husband managed to produce such beautiful things. How lovely the children looked, the boy in particular.

'Don't you think Ryan looks a lot like you did at his age?' said Ben.

'How old is he?'

'Seven, next month. Don't you think he does?' All David could see was how perfect Ryan looked at only seven years old.

A couple of days later, while Ben and he were having breakfast, voices could be heard at the front door.

'Where is he?' a girl asked. This was followed by the sound of running feet. Two children chased round the corner and almost skidded to a halt. They stood very close; she, a little way back, but he almost touching David's knee with his tummy. Not having done this before, David decided to try and respond to their greeting. As he turned to face them, a little pair of hands reached for his neck. Copying the gesture, David hugged Ryan and lifted him up to screams of delight and laughter. Lynda, not wanting to miss out on the fun, instinctively threw herself towards him and wrapped her body around his thigh. Improvising, David thought he was doing well and noticed how different they were to him. They simply responded with how they felt.

These two energetic souls wanted all his attention. Ryan won and told him all about his life; mainly about school, his gang and his girlfriend, who he said was the strongest in the school. At this point their mother, who had been standing behind, shook her head, mouthing silently with a grotesque stretching of her face.

'I don't know why he likes her.'

'I think she's quite cute,' added Ben. 'A bit of a tomboy though.'

Ryan went on to tell of someone else, a boy called 'Little Jamie,' who was in the 'littlest-class,' and that he loved him. As he spoke, his face was so close to David's. He seemed to have no notion of physical boundaries, or perhaps he didn't care. How close should he have stood? Should his breath have been felt against David's lips? How long should he have looked into someone else's eyes, without laughing, or making faces, or making fun of David for looking right back? Ryan was more honest than anyone he had met before, he made David love him for this.

The third time that David saw Ryan was on the weekend, having been invited for tea. Climbing on to David's lap, his nephew insisted on kissing his face. He rubbed his head into David's chest, squirming and shifting his body. Ryan's affection was unchecked and relentless. The soft little-boy lips whispered into David's ear, tickling and seducing him with his innocence. David felt his dick swelling. It got hard, a healthy, persistent, rock hard. Not wanting Ryan to notice, David manoeuvered him off his knee.

'Come and watch me play the piano,' said Ryan.

'I'll follow you in a minute,' replied David, trying to cover up the bulge in his jeans. David was wearing boxer shorts which didn't help, so he had to wait before standing.

'Come, watch me,' insisted Ryan.

'No, I can't.'

'Why not?' asked Judy, who'd been platting Lynda's hair.

'Because look at my dick,' was the truth, but 'Give me a minute,' was what he said. He tried to give Judy a look of slight exhaustion, needing time to collect himself. David wasn't sure what the movement of muscles on his face suggested. But something was understood, enough to get Judy to deal with Ryan.

'Come on, practice with me and then we'll show Uncle David.'

Left sitting in the kitchen, David had time to think about what was happening. He was aware his responses were complex, even sinister; but, almost grudgingly, he also realised how nice he felt.

Later, during dinner, Ryan asked many questions.

'Do you go to the gym? Can I go with you? Can I feel your muscles? Can I look at your tummy?

With a nod of approval from mum, David gave in, stood, and pulled up his T-shirt.

'That's not like daddy's,' said Ryan, staring, with his mouth open wide and his spoon resting sideways between his gappy teeth. He reached up, without thinking, without asking, without knowing better and rubbed his young hands over the ridges of David's perfect abdomen.

'Daddy's fat,' he said with a giggle, slowly fingering in between the bumps, still not taking his hand away, lingering. Finally, as he withdrew, Ryan smiled. David presumed it might have some relation to him. To something tactile, physical, or male.

David told Ryan about Flora and invited him down to London to see the Christmas lights. 'Really! At Christmas?' Ryan's response was complete wonder. He counted using his fingers, mouthing the numbers. The whole of his body swung from side to side. Then he jumped up and down saying, 'That's five months away.' Feelings fluttered in David's tummy, as though a hand were opening inside him. He was looking forward to Christmas as much as Ryan now.

Reviewing the day's events, David realised his infatuation with his nephew. Ryan, with his sticking-out-at-all-angles-hair looked at David like no one ever had. An instinctive boy who seemed to know how to treat him, seemed to know what he needed. Surely it was natural to be turned on by such affection. Ryan simply loved David because he was his uncle. Whereas David loved his nephew for his openness and trust.

David burst out laughing at the thought of trying to explain his feelings to Judy. Even with the most theoretical and very best communication, he could guess at her response. Ryan would not be allowed to visit him at Christmas.

BOUNDLESS

A new "Sent" ad was being screened. The same female model, that was in the previous ad, sat in profile, at the left hand side of the frame. Her curly auburn hair vibrated against the turquoise of the background. Her hands were delicate, with fingers that looked stretched. Her nail varnish was a rust colour.

A tarantula dissolved onto the right of the screen. The woman, beckoned it. As the spider crawled towards her, the speed of the film increased, making it look clockwork and manic. She clicked her fingers, and magically it vanished.

Joe clasped his hands. To the editor, this meant Joe liked what he had seen.

A deadly coral snake appeared. Again she beckoned, it slithered, she clicked, and it too vanished. Finally, a pale green bottle of "Sent" perfume dissolved onto the screen. When beckoned, the atomiser released a living mist. This covered the model.

The camera turned in fast motion. It stopped dramatically, viewing the model face on, with the perfume in front. A glint of light caught the small etched writing. This expanded, bleaching the colour from the screen, until only a stain was left. This pulsed until there was nothing but white.

'Perfect,' he whispered, 'absolutely perfect.'

The editor contained a grin. Joe looked at him, then quickly back to the monitor, not wanting to miss a second. 'You're a genius.'

The film froze for three seconds. Then a voice, slowly said.

'Sent from where?'

'That timing, I love it. I'll say it again Bill, you're a genius.'

'They're your ideas. I just make them work.'

'I don't care. All I know is, that's beautiful.'

Bill leaned back in his chair and put his feet up.

'Where do you get your ideas from Joe?'

'What, this?'

'Yes this, and everything else. I caught your exhibition.'

'You should see a doctor.'

'Shut up, idiot. You're an artist Joe, and a bloody good one.'

'Is there any such thing?'

'What do you mean?'

'Well, who decides what's good?'

'I don't know.' Bill took out a cigarette, still focused on the question. 'Galleries? People who buy it, I guess.'

'You mean, anyone who has a vested interest.'

'That's a bit negative.'

'I think it's more negative to convince some people that they're not artists.'

'So you think anyone can do it?'

'Yeah.'

'There's no way of judging?'

'No.' Joe paused. 'I prefer work by friends.'

'And if I gave you a choice between a Bill Fletcher and a Van Gogh.'

'I said, friends, stupid.'

Bill tried to nudge Joe with his foot and fell out of his chair.

'Thanks for the vote of confidence, mate.'

'Anytime,' said Joe, looking at his watch. 'I've got to go. Love you for this, I won't forget it.'

'So marry me then,' said Bill, settling back into his chair. Joe was already on his way out of the room.

FREEDOM

Stopping his motor-bike outside the gym, Joe honked. He was dressed in his leathers and looked very sexy. There were a group of men, inside the doorway. David stood separately. One of the men smiled at Joe, who nodded in response.

'Know him?' said David.

'Probably.'

'Stud,' said David and rolled his eyes. Joe revved his engine loud. 'Do you have to do that?'

'No,' said Joe, laughing. 'But I like to.'

'It's big.'

'It's a road bike,' said Joe, proud but casual.

David clambered on, feeling a prissy, but hoping he was pulling off the image. He knew he was being watched.

'All set?' asked Joe. Then he slapped the side of his leg and cried, 'Yahoo!'

It didn't take long before they were out of the city. Green grass, brown walls, blue sky blurred beside them. At first, David kept his visor up, until they picked up speed. His breathing became noisy, trapped, along with a smile of approval, safe within the helmet.

Joe got off on the roar of the engine, and having David cuddled up behind him. Loving every inch and second of the journey, he twisted on the throttle and drove.

They headed towards the coast, arriving within the hour. Just like when David was small, in the back of his parents' car, the first sight of the glittering sea made his eyes enlarge. He squeezed his driver's waist, and Joe patted his leg in acknowledgement. David breathed in the clean air. What a great idea it was, to get out of the city. Away from the din, the dead air, the contorted streets and smiles.

Pulling into a cobbled alleyway, close to the promenade, they parked and headed straight for the pier. It was Monday, off season, so the pavements were empty. On the pier, they leaned over the side and watched the waves hitting the rusty iron supports. They walked, then leaned some more. Seagulls swooped out of the sky to catch food thrown by a couple of children. Sitting on a bench, they stared out onto the ceaseless, exhausted, ancient waves.

'Don't they ever get sick of sloshing?' asked David, whilst letting his mind go free.

'Who?' said Joe. Then, realising what he meant. 'Well first, it's not they. It's all one thing. It's always done the same thing and always will. It's about accepting what you are.'

'Uhm.'

'Do you ever get sick of what you are?'

'Truthfully, yes.'

'When?'

'Like now. Well, not now this second, but recently.'

'Are you sure it's not the parcel that's making you feel uneasy?'

'Maybe. It really makes you wonder about everything you do and say. Who did I offend? Is it about my lifestyle, or is it my fucking hair.'

'It's obviously got to you. This might be what they wanted.'

'What are you saying? Should I ignore it?'

'No, I don't think you should pretend it never happened. But, just try and not let it get to you. I know this is easier said than done.'

'You're telling me.'

'But that's what we're doing today, getting away from it, having a change of scenery.'

'Joe, for a man, you're very thoughtful.'

'No. I'm not. I just wanted you to myself all day.'

'I'm all for that.'

'Me too.'

Joe played with his fingers, then held then up.

'What?' said David, knowing well, the sign Joe made, meant something.

'It's sign language.'

'And what does it mean?'

Joe held his little finger, his forefinger and thumb straight out, with the two in the middle held as a fist. With his other hand Joe pointed out the words.

'Look, this is *I*,' he said pointing to his little finger. 'This is an *L*,' following the line from the tip of his forefinger down to the base of his thumb, then up to the top of it. 'And this is a *Y*,' he said joining all three together.

'I, L, Y?' said David.

'No. I love you. I use it for *like* though'

'God, you're corny.'

'But you wouldn't have it any other way.'

'Something like that.'

Clouds of silver, white and pink, hovered on the brink of rain, or perhaps of clearing up. Beside the pier, a rickety fair ground tried hard to be happy. It looked as though it was about to sigh and stop. After years of repainting and turning on aching cogs, its spangle had gone. Joe and David decided there were a couple of rides worth bothering with; the Waltzers which weren't thrilling and the Ferris wheel which had a soothing effect.

They played tag with the shore. It made them children again, which they liked. Tired and hungry they found a place to eat, then decided to head home. On the bike again, David felt reassured. All he had to do was hold on to Joe until he got back home.

Amber flashes divided black sky overhead. Cats' eyes guided. Red tail-lights reminded them there were other people in the world. By the time they got back to London their bodies had settled. Clay-like, David got off the bike.

'Thanks Joe.'

'It was my pleasure.' David had helmet-hair, which he attempted to sort out, but gave up. 'Don't worry, you look good.'

'I think I'm too tired to care.'

Joe got ready to leave. 'I'll give you a call tomorrow.'

'Okay.'

Inside the apartment, Flora sat, more waiting than reading.

All David could muster was, 'Are you coming to bed?'

'I'll just finish this chapter,' said Flora not looking up.

CRUSH

Beautiful days aren't just about weather and setting. They are a feeling, an attitude. Hyde Park was the setting; the coffee house near the rose gardens. It is a place which succeeds in encouraging the feeling of aloneness. Nature in the city often fails, looking quaint and cheap.

Even though it was quite cool, Flora and David sat outside to take in their surroundings.

'Sing for me,' said Flora. Then she paused, as though changing the direction of her thoughts, 'I love it when you sing for me.'

David looked up and tried to smile; but, realising that it wasn't real, made a silly face, just enough to make Flora smile.

'Sing that song.' Again, her mind twisted, unsure and insecure. 'You're not going to, are you?'

David didn't raise his head this time, but mouthed "no."

'You and Joe have fun yesterday? A boy's day out, hey?'

'There just wasn't room on the bike for you.'

'I would of got in the way.'

Quietly, 'That's not true.'

'Do you still like me?' This was half joking, but the half that wasn't seemed desperate. David didn't answer. He couldn't take it seriously.

'Do you?'

'Yes!' he said, with a sadness in his voice. He tried to change the conversation, 'How's your coffee?'

'It's our sex life, isn't it?.'

More resigned, 'I think it's complicated.'

A breeze blew through the park. High in the trees, branches swayed. The couple were showered with a sweet smelling dust. Stillness returned.

'Sometimes you're so cold,' said Flora.

'That's not allowed?'

'If you like me, you like me.'

A ladybug landed on Flora's coat. David reached over to lift it off, but Flora swatted it. David recoiled in shock.

'What are you doing?' said Flora.

'Nothing baby.'

'You are allowed to touch me. If you want to, that is.'

David extended his arm again and rested his hand on Flora's.

'Stop! I don't want to have to ask you.'

'You don't. I like touching you.'

'Don't do it to please me.'

'I do like to please you.'

'What about you? What do you want?' David didn't answer, he couldn't. 'Do you care about what I'm saying?'

'Yes.' He sighed. Not out of boredom, but he'd had enough of the conversation.

'Well what do you want?'

'I want to stop fighting.'

'You just can't be bothered, can you?'

'You know how much I...' David stopped. It felt wrong, having to spell things out. He did it anyway. 'I love you.'

'It's hard to say, isn't it?

'Sometimes.'

'I knew it. You don't give a fuck, do you?'

'I just can't switch on at your command. Sometimes I feel more than others.'

'Yeah, at first you felt more, and now less and less.' David raised his eyes looking for the thing to say that would stop the attack. 'What are you thinking?' He didn't answer. 'Quickly. What are you holding from me? The whole idea of asking, is that you don't censor - so that I might hear the truth, not something you've edited to please me. What were you thinking?'

David had to stop looking at Flora. All he saw was anger and hatred. The kind that came from caring about someone.

'You're not even listening are you?'

'I'm listening to you.' He stared at the grass in front of him. 'Would you like some biscuits?'

'Is that what you've been thinking about all this time? You haven't been listening to a word I've said.'

A fly landed on Flora.

'For God's sake, these bloody bugs. They must think I'm shit or something.'

'They think you're a flower. They love you.' He made a bug face and tried to kiss Flora.

'How cute!' she said, annoyed.

David tickled her. Reluctantly, she laughed.

'How about those biscuits?' he said.

'Lamb. Why won't you ever talk anything through?'

David looked away, determined to end the conversation. He got up to go into the cafe.

'If they have shortbread, shall I get you some?'

'Please. But I do want to finish this when you get back.'

David saluted, 'Aye-ye, Captain.'

'Are we still on for the theatre next week?'

'Sure. The National?'

'Great. Just you and me.'

As he walked away he looked back. Flora was being bothered by some litter that had stuck to her shoe. A fool would have been able to see that he cared for her, or at least felt for her.

GRANDMOTHER

Sunlight filled the room. This bleached the surfaces it could and gave hazy edges to the rest. An old woman sat at the window. She smiled at her neighbour, who entered the house next door. Out of sight of passers by, beneath the sill, she checked her nails. They were clean and short. Dipping the tips of her fingers into some Vaseline, she gently rubbed the arse of a baby, lying in its crib.

Everything was perfect. The blankets were soft and powder blue. The old woman smiled. She blew, and a stream of smell connected with her grandson. The baby smiled back, his tongue filling the space between his lips. His grandmother waved to a girl walking her dog, she kept her other hand on his arse.

A bird flew down from a chestnut tree in the garden and stood singing on the sill. If I were more able, thought the old woman, I would reach out, and the dear creature might hop on to my finger. Its little head would be so close to my ear. Maybe it would sing a pretty song just for me. She sighed, then a smile broke out on her face. Her front tooth stayed resting on the edge of her lip as she was dragged back to her youth. Rolling down a hill, daisies flashed by. White clouds, then blue sky. She saw a blur of grass, then white and blue, before she tumbled to the bottom of the hill. Bent double, she laughed with her friends. They were happy, and loved each other. Jumping up, they skipped back to the top of the hill. Rolling again, blue sky smeared. Daisies coughed blood onto her red gingham dress.

Whether it was her age or just who she had become, she daydreamed often. This was something she checked herself on, sometimes. Other times she let herself go, reminiscing for minutes, enjoying fantasies for longer. She would sit staring onto a wall, seeing far beyond its surface.

Barely able to return the smile given by a neighbour, she dragged herself more to her present life. She could hear herself crying in her - then life. She waved. If she had stayed back there a second longer, she would - with a smile on her face - have cried on her birthday.

It was spring. Grass smells were sweet and healing. The old woman sniffed at the air, acknowledging everything it had to offer. Letting her hand slide, she allowed her little finger to massage the edge of the baby's arse hole. An adult might squirm when having this done, might arch and stretch, might sigh and close their eyes. David gurgled, making bubbles with his mouth. Waving his plump little hands in the air he reached for a hug.

His father liked to put cuddly toys into the crib. David would push them away as best he could. He would cry. Then his father would back off and his mother would feed him, or burp him, or do some other thing.

The old woman had on her favorite dress. It was a special day. Looking around at all the cards on the fireplace, she was reminded that she was getting older, but also that she was loved a great deal. She looked down at David. You're so perfect, she thought, so unaffected. All you know is how you feel and you don't care why. 'I love you so much,' she said out loud. Then faintly, she sang, 'My-little-little-little-little-lovely-boy.'

Distracted by some commotion in the garden, the old woman squinted, attempting to focus her eyes. The bird tugged at a worm in the ground. There followed a pitiful fight, which ended with the worm breaking in two. It flailed in its captor's beak, glistening in the sunlight. The bird hopped and took flight.

INSIDE

My vision is bleary as I open the kitchen drawer. I take out the tablets and pour four disks into my hand. They are too large to swallow, but can be chewed, or dissolved in water. This morning I chew them. It's quicker and I want to get back to bed. It's best to grind them with a mouthful of water, to create a solution. If you're not careful they get stuck in your back teeth. Their taste is a mixture of artificial sweetener and a chemical additive. The absorption is better if there is no acid in the stomach, so either two hours after food, or on an empty stomach, is recommended. This drug is used to slow down the replication of H.I.V. in my body. I take it along with three other drugs. When I started on medication, I felt nauseous to begin with, but this went away within a couple of weeks. Taking medication is boring, but I think it's worth it. I feel as though I might outlive this disease.

 I brush my teeth, trying not to wake up, keeping my eyes not fully open and unfocused. I pretend that I'm not awake yet, and that this isn't what I'll have to do for the rest of my life. Hey, so what, I'll have to go the the toilet, eat and sleep for the rest of my life too. Surely I can handle a little more "have to." Okay, a lot more "have to." The thing is, if I don't do it this way - get up, take them and go back to bed - then, the alternative is to get up, take them and then wait half an hour, before eating. Again, so that stomach acids don't effect the medication. I find, waiting a half hour before eating in the morning is horrible. So, my pretending not to be awake routine is how it is for now. That is, until I have to switch to another drug, if, rather when, this one begins to be less effective. When, that is, my resourceful virus develops a resistant strain to my current medication.

 Dragging my feet back to bed, I try to convince myself I'm still asleep; but I take in too much, that wakes me too much (letters have to be mailed, my diary has to be looked at, appointments may as well be kept). I try to get back to my dream. As though the pictures, or the memories of them, will make me believe I'm in there, sleeping again. I do remember the images. I begin to cling to them. Then, I remember the whole of the dream: I was preempting my getting up, with a neurotic plan of action - maybe to soften the harshness of the real event, or maybe to try to dream it so that I wouldn't have to really do it.

I get into bed and close my eyes. But, no matter how hard I try, all I can feel is hunger. I open my eyes. It's ten minutes, then fifteen, then seventeen minutes from when I just lay down. When twenty-eight nagging minutes are finally through, knowing that it will take the last couple to pour out my cereal, I get up. I can't help wondering when it says "half an hour before food," do they mean, to the second.

ROMANCE

'It's just down there on your left,' came a voice from behind. David turned around to find a woman standing in the rain, with no umbrella, nor even a coat.

The sky rained huge drops that knocked noisily against the skin. The wind seemed purposeful, as though on a mission. David hailed cab after cab. All were full. He was getting too wet to care. He gave in and looked up. The rain felt good on his face, his lips, his closed eyes. He enjoyed the experience, like he hadn't done since he was a child.

'It's just down there on your left. The taxi-rank, I mean.' By turning and facing Flora, David allowed their relationship to begin.

Flora had been in no hurry, she had no one to go home to, no one to care if she went home at all - wet or dry, late or early. She had decided to sit out the storm. Alone she had gone into a restaurant and alone she had ordered food. There was nothing sad about this, except that it wasn't what she really wanted. What she did want was love.

Whilst waiting for her food to arrive, Flora had stared out of the window. A man caught her eye, whom she recognised from the gym. She had watched him and liked him. So she seized the opportunity. Putting down her fork, she lifted her napkin off her lap and, without her coat, she made her way outside.

'Its just down there on your left. The taxi-rank, I mean. I don't think you'll get one now, there'll be lots of people waiting.' From the look on David's face, Flora knew to continue. 'Alternatively,' she said, avoiding his eyes, looking at the ground. 'You could join me for dinner. I'm just in here.' Flora gestured behind her. 'The food's fine. I mean.' Her eyes rose to his. 'Would you join me, please?'

David saw a woman, whose wet hair was sweetly unflattering, and whose blouse stuck to her skin and bra. From the definite tone of her voice, and the expressions he could read through the water on her face, he made decisions. About how sincere she might be, how caring she might be to him. If he gave her a chance. If he took a chance, by going into the restaurant with her.

'Madame! Madame!' came the waiter's voice from the doorway.

'Yes, I'm coming... Would you?' she said, whilst blowing the rain off her nose.

They went inside, they ate, they talked and liked each other. Numbers were exchanged and a date arranged.

David had always been good to look at, right from the crib. He was aware that he got special treatment. What was harder to work out was, whether people wanted to know him, be him, or fuck him.

Flora had not been so lucky with her looks. Her face was a little long and her skin a touch bumpy. But, being guileful, she knew how to treat the handsome. Having watched David whilst working out, she saw how he responded when others came on to him. It didn't take long before she knew what he did and didn't like. When they finally connected there were two different things happening - David was responding naturally and Flora was acting naturally. She didn't think this was evil. How else could she attract a man as pretty as David. Using her brains seemed no more manipulative to her than someone using their looks.

'What do you do for a living?' David asked.

'I design buildings, well parts of them.'

'What kind?'

'Usually they're conversions. I concentrate on "special needs." Access for wheelchairs. That kind of thing.'

Flora and David's relationship consisted of getting used to each other's habits, and not asking too many questions. David believed he loved Flora in the same way people believe they love God. It doesn't have to be questioned. Believing you believe is how it's held together. So when David got Joe alone, and said to him quite timidly, 'I think there's something wrong.' It wouldn't be a surprise for those who thought love was something different.

WHORE

'Hot, sexy show. Do you want to see a sexy show?'

Barely lit horny men wanked and grinned. Greasy face marks smudged the glass barrier. It steamed as customers tried to get closer, whilst avoiding closeness of any kind. During Joe's shifts at the strip show, coins were put into slots and cum into tissues. He'd been looked at too many times in a way that wasn't caring. He'd also been touched in too many ways that weren't about being kind. Twenty one years old, and Joe was already use to being used.

By twenty two he was working in a brothel. He'd only been there four months when he was put in charge of running it whilst the owner went on holiday. The place got raided. Joe was arrested. Could a whore tell the truth? No. Joe was sent to prison.

Noises. Relentless layers of sound. The shifting of bodies, breathing men, rustles, cracks, coughs and voices. Sharp whispers, barely there, to you, about you, and you yourself. This was constant so you were never alone. Traffic could be heard in a distant street, a reminder that there was a world outside your cell. This was a consolation.

Home, for Joe, was a room nine feet by seven, including a toilet, continually giving off its smell, a sink that sometimes had hot water and a bed with someone imaginary in it, waiting. Joe laid in that same bed, with those same cotton sheets and blanket - day in, day out . He created a lover, their gender fluid, who had all the body parts and sensitivity needed. Joe became expert with his hands, a vehicle for his lover. Ordinarily, when leading a life he chose, Joe had sex appeal. But, that light had been switched out for now. His authentic smile, calm disposition, and solid smooth physique, were not available.

A social worker might say Joe showed signs of unsocial behavior. They might presume there had been a recent bereavement. They'd be correct. Joe grieved for the person he wasn't allowed to be here. The next step might be to guess a history of abuse, for that's often the next step. If, at this point, Joe said 'Fuck off!' This might be read as anti social behavior, which it was; but, if understood better, it might be clear he was tired, lifelessly tired, of those who make decisions about other people's fates. Sickened by those who control morality as though they had the right, as if they always got it right.

Out of boredom Joe itemized ideas and memories. He used himself as nourishment. Deconstructing thoughts, he manipulated them, flipped them, made them opposite to what they had been. Evil, good, and the smear in between, seemed to be a structureless weave. Without this understanding, he would not have been able to make sense of his situation. There would only have been a void in his prison.

Too many decisions were made whilst inside for Joe to waste further time. When first out, he got Income Support from the state. He worked at the peepshow again, just long enough to afford some decent clothes, a comfortable flat and the memories that came with the job. He joined an escort agency and began to collect his favorite customers, those who were wealthy and influential but, more importantly, those who were kind. The agency cut was high and they made him feel he had obligations. He left. Moved on.

Next, Joe placed an ad. It wasn't long before he knew how to work his customers. He'd have them drooling but never getting off. Not before they visited and he got paid. There were some who liked to worship Joe, his torso and his hard round bum. Others hated him. Sex wasn't what they wanted, but an exercise of power, a channel for their other frustrations and anger.

A change of direction came, with a customer called Rick Derrybunce. He was sweet and powerful, and worked in television advertising. Joe asked if he could read over scripts and presentations for ads. Next, he drew up treatments of his own. Rick realised Joe was talented and started taking him more seriously. In six months, Joe learned a great deal. Finally, with a lot of persuasion, Rick let him submit a few ideas for some minor accounts. Out of the first six he put in for, he got five. It was freelance work through a production company. Within three months he was asked to join them full-time. Joe built an impressive showreel and made good contacts. After two years, he was freelancing again. This time round, it was different.

More and more Joe found himself becoming absorbed in creative pastimes, painting, sculpture, writing, anything. Anything that kept him away from others. Alone and safe.

SADO-MASOCHISM

An electric junction box with wires attached, sits on a table. Beside it, there is a bench with a central pivot. For the moment, it's locked in place. A man, the recipient, is strapped down. He has a redhead's complexion, his skin a pale blue tinge.

There is a ticking sound. Louder than a clock, possibly a metronome, pacing the space, dividing the time, which otherwise would be abstracted. Time is now based on the course of events, that's all. The ticking simply reminds the recipient that time is passing. Things are moving, not necessarily forward, but in some direction. One thing will definitely lead to another, then another, and another, as sure as there was day and night, before entering this room. The pulse of the room consumes the body's beat, the tiny life rhythm that once was his.

Metal pins have been pushed through the recipient's nipples and another through his navel. A triangle of conductive points, focusing the torso, are connected via the junction box to the mains. At first the twitch of the electric current tingles. But, as it is increased, the sensation is more like a crack, then more like a strike. Imagine the sensation of tensing your muscles and how painful this can be. Then imagine these muscles tensed so tight that they engrave lines into your innards. This is your meat, cutting into itself, ceasing only when the voltage is released.

What more control could you have over someone than to get underneath their skin and grasp at their insides? Letting go when you want. Only then, giving him back to himself. Until you again make him yours. How whimsical and powerful. What a perfect betrayal of the natural way of things. Possession and not possession and not. At the flick of a switch and the turn of a dial, possess a lot, possess even more.

'You have received a level six. What is the most you think you can take?'

'Eight.' So this is administered. Like a fish wanting life-giving water, the man convulses. The current subsides as instantly as it begins.

An addition is brought to this scene. A bulbous shaped dildo, with screws at the base and a foil strip winding around the shaft to the tip. The head of this, is pushed against the sphincter. With massaging, the muscle begins to give way, then to open, then to desire. In time, it begins to crave intrusion. The dildo slides slowly into the arse, stretching the membrane lining. The recipient groans, as his arse stretches over the widest point of the dildo. Then, the muscles close up around the neck, trapping it inside. The screws at the base are connected, with wire, to the junction box. And in turn, to the other points which dissect the upper body.

The contractions are titillating to begin with, stimulating the prostate. With each twist of the dial the sensation compounds, until it's as though a spirit lives within this body; pulling at limbs, folding organs, manipulating his skin from beneath. The blood in the recipient's veins seems to stop, turn and go backwards, away from his heart, round the wrong way. Then, it changes and goes back again. Each time ripping against the walls, all the walls, of the stomach, the brain and his covering flesh. It rejects, then receives. Over and over again, until there is a break from it all, possession is stopped.

Lying panting, goose-pimply hot and cold. Solitude, comfort and normality steadily return.

'Please can I try a level nine,' says the recipient.

In the shadows within the room, corners round themselves and disappear. Black walls look sweaty because of their sheen. They stare down upon this ticking, moaning, pleading sight. There is a single window up in the roof, where condensation coats the glass. Every drop of water reflects this scene. Countless blobs of masochism trickle in thin streams, while the action continues, going further at times, oblivious to, but because of the society outside.

FINCH

David had been trying to distract himself by pretending to clean the kitchen. Joe had just arrived after being called half an hour before. Now they both sat looking at the parcel that had arrived in the morning post.

The front door opened and closed. Flora walked into the kitchen with two big portfolios under her arms. 'How's my Lambski?' Then when she saw the parcel. 'Oh.'

'Yeah. Oh,' said David.

'I don't think it's going anywhere,' she said. 'Why don't we have a coffee.'

'I think it's creepy,' said Joe

'Coffee's not so creepy?'

David seemed more tired than upset. 'Ha, ha.'

'Look at this,' said Joe. 'The frank mark. It's from here in the city.'

Flora filled the kettle. 'Well done, but have you noticed the writings different.'

'Hell, you remember that?' said David.

'Well only that it was much larger. I thought it looked odd on such a small package.'

'Yeah, I remember now. God, you're good at this.'

'Be careful how you open it,' said Flora. 'There could be anything inside, a bomb, a rat...'

As she tried to think of another example, David cut her off. 'Okay. Okay. I get the picture.'

'Sorry.'

'Whoever said *I* was going to open it anyway?'

'Are you thinking of just leaving it there?' said Flora.

'No,' said David. Then, looking up at Joe, 'I thought maybe...'

'I don't think so young man,' said Joe.

Flora's mind was somewhere else. Eleven years old and watching her father. As he had always done, he opened his birthday presents with not the slightest bit of joy. Was it that he knew what he was going to get - slippers, shaving stuff, Dad-stuff? Or did he really not enjoy spending time with his family? Could he take no pleasure in pretending he didn't know what was inside the obvious-shaped packages? Was he jaded - so adult - that he couldn't stop himself from tearing the corner of each gift and, when seeing no surprise, putting the thing on the floor without bothering to finish unwrapping it. Everyone noticed. Mum rolled her eyes in resignation. Flora saw disappointment. She felt embarrassed that she hadn't cared to make more of an effort. She questioned the child she was meant to be. The one who'd bought what she felt was the right thing to buy and who'd used every penny she'd had. Flora was confused by her father's response. Where was the good bit in this. Why was no one happy with what had happened. Where was the love?

'We could take it to the police station,' suggested David.

'And what if it's drugs?' said Flora.

Joe feigned shock. 'Is that likely?'

Flora seemed a little impatient. 'I just don't think they'd be that interested in our postal problems.'

'It's more than that,' said David. 'Isn't it?'

Seeing such uneasiness Joe said boldly, 'I think we should see what it is.'

'And, if it's you-know-what,' said Flora, wafting her nose with her hand.

'Then we'll...' David seemed uncomfortable. 'We'll try and get the post office to put a block on parcels or something.'

Flora got a knife from the drawer and hesitantly handed it to David. He squirmed as he remembered the previous event. Carefully, he cut around the tape which neatly sealed the box. 'Anal tape work,' he said, only catching both meanings afterwards. He paused.

'Here goes.' Slowly he peeled back the lid. There was a plastic bag inside, tied in a knot at the top.

'What is it? What is it?'

'I can't tell.'

Flora took hold of the top of the bag and gently lifted it out. 'Ugh!'

Lying in blood was a tiny finch. It looked as though its head had been pulled off, barely attached by a vein.

'Get me a newspaper,' said Flora. David did as he was told.

'There's more,' he said, as he reached inside the box and pulled out a note. It read, "Watch your back, pretty-boy."

'Well, at least they think you're pretty.'

'For God's sake Flora!'

'I was just trying to make him feel better,' she said in defense.

'Don't talk about me as though I'm not here,' said David.

'Sorry baby. You're the boss.'

'How patronizing,' said Joe.

'Mind your own business,' said Flora.

'It is my business.'

'This is my apartment and my life.'

'What the fuck are you saying?'

'These didn't start arriving till you...' Flora stopped herself.

'What were you going to say?'

'Nothing.'

Feeling contempt, but also hurt, Joe stared at Flora, glanced at David and then put his head down. 'I've got to go.'

'Don't go,' said David. 'Don't let him go.'

'Yeah. I'm sorry.'

'I really should go. I'm starving.'

'Where are you going to go?' said David.

'Wherever.'

David looked at Flora.

'Go with him, if you want to. You don't need my permission.'

'I wasn't asking for it. I thought you might want to come.'

Flora focused somewhere in front of her. 'I don't think so. You boys run along.'

Joe winced at her terminology. 'Are you coming, *boy*?' he said to David.

In the car David and Joe sat in silence for a while, each going over their version of what had happened. Their argument had distracted them from the parcel. Slowly, Joe calmed.

'Where do you want to go sweetheart?' he said.
'Away from here.'
'Sounds good to me.'
'I'm probably reacting far too dramatically to all this,' said David. 'What do you think?'
'How ever you react is probably the best way for you.'
'You sound like a therapist.'
'Sorry.'
'I've never seen you annoyed before.'
'Well get used to it.' Joe pretended to scowl, then smiled.
'She doesn't seem to take it seriously, the parcels.'
'I'm sure she does. It's probably just her way of dealing with it. I imagine she's worried too.'
'Do you think?'
'Yeah. She is human.'
'I guess so.'
Again, there was silence. They each thought about the argument.
'The note called you "Pretty-boy." Is this a name anyone has used for you before.'
'Lots of people have called me pretty.' David looked awkward. 'But I can't remember anyone using it like a name.'
'It sounds bitter.'
'I know.'
'Are you scared?'
'Do you think I should be?' said David, looking more serious. 'I'm confused, stressed, paranoid. Take your pick.'
Joe pulled over outside Wok Wok in the Fulham Road. 'Listen,' he said. 'Maybe you should come and stay at my house for a little while. You might feel safer.'
'You do think it's serious.'
'I'm not saying that.'
'No. Maybe you're right,' said David. His eyes darted as his mind flicked thoughts.' I feel so pathetic.
'No. You're a shining star. That's all I see.' Joe cupped his hand on David's cheek. David's head relaxed into Joe's fatherly and calming gesture. 'So it's settled?'
'I'll see what Flora thinks.'

'Of course.'

After eating. Joe drove David home. 'I don't think I'll come in.'

'Don't continue it Joe.'

'I'm already over it. I'll send her some flowers tomorrow. I just want to get home.'

'You're a good man Joe.'

'Yeah, yeah, yeah. Get out of my car you soppy bugger.'

David had never met a man as caring as Joe. Also, he had never met any woman, who made him feel the way Joe did.

RAPE

It was simply a case of carrying on with daily life. Worrying did no good. David did have a bad feeling about the parcels. The three friends talked about their possible fears and joked.

David had a casting for a movie the following morning. A good night's sleep was essential so he planned to be in bed by eleven. He left his friends at the restaurant after dinner. On the way home he thought about Joe and Flora. They had gone to dinner in a rough part of town. What if someone were waiting for them? What if they had been followed? Flora was the most important person in David's life and Joe was quickly taking second place. Whoever sent the parcels must know who he was close to. They would be an obvious target. Why hadn't they thought about this before, or taken precautions? David became annoyed. He decided to call the restaurant and warn them.

By the time he got home the telephone was the only thing on his mind. He dialed the number and it rang repeatedly. Suddenly a knife was pushed against David's neck. A hand stifled his gasp. 'Don't move a muscle, or I'll cut it out,' whispered a voice.

David froze, trying to control his breathing.

'You're going to keep quiet. Do you hear?' The hand that covered his mouth released finger by finger. 'Good boy.' This same hand crept down to David's fly and undid his jeans. 'Good.' He took hold of David's balls and twisted them. Within a second, the knife at his neck was repositioned under his balls. 'Now you're going to make this easy for me, aren't you?' David's trousers were pulled down. He was bent over. 'Show me your cunt Aidsy queer. That's right. Sweet! Yeah. Sweet. Do you know what I'm going to do to you?' He tightened the grip on David's balls. 'Do you?' David tried to answer but couldn't. 'I can't hear you queer.'

David tried to say 'no,' although it was more of a whine.

Spit landed on the base of David's spine and dribbled down the crack of his arse.

'If you don't make this real easy for me,' said the man, 'I'm going to open you up with my blade. Do you understand?'

'Yes.'

A thick finger pushed into David's arse. He felt excruciating pain. A dick forced in. Then it pulled out abruptly. It went in and out only a few times. Cum shot inside David's arse. Time changed speed. David fell to the ground, landing slowly. His face was kicked. The face which smiled so easily turned inside out. On each blow, a little more of it hit the carpet. The man had fun. He kicked the arse repeatedly he'd just been fucking.

He pulled off David's watch and stuck it inside him. 'Can you tell what time is it boy?' Using his fingers, he managed to stick his dick in after it. He pissed. 'Bet your cunt feels nice and warm now...eh?' He pulled out, stood up and tried to walk on David. He fell. For a moment, he became tender, kissing and stroking the lifeless heap. Then he kicked David again and continued his assault. Time must have been still now, for this went on and on, until a break from the violence lasted.

Up to this point, David at least had the comfort that he would not survive. Now fear took hold of what was left of his conscious mind. Pain reminded him he was still alive. The phone had fallen to the floor. He could reach it. The line was dead. It had been pulled from the wall. Blood glued him to the floor, heavy and wet. He got to the hall, then to the lift and finally to the entrance, where he lay, half in and half out of this world. Mist kissed David, settling on his face. Time was now the speed of water trickling over broken lips, there was little else.

SAFETY

Seconds after David fell, he was spotted by a woman on security, patrolling the building. She dragged him inside where it was warmer, then called an ambulance. David was taken to Charing Cross Hospital.

Flora and Joe sat patiently in the waiting room. Eventually, they were told David was sleeping and could be seen. They were led by a nurse to a room. The lights were dimmed. It was quiet but for a deep slow breathing. Made comfortable with morphine, David had found peace.

'Is he okay?' said Flora.
'Yes,' said the nurse.
'Is he in pain?' said Joe.
'No. He's heavily sedated.'
'When will be able to come home?' said Joe
'Not just yet. He...' The nurse stopped.
'What?' said Joe.
'He had to have some stitches, around his anus.'
'Oh my God,' said Joe.
'Why?' said Flora.
Again the nurse hesitated. 'The doctor believes he may have been sexually assaulted.'
'Why in God's name?' said Flora.
'My poor baby,' said Joe.

The nurse suggested that they go home and get a good night's sleep. There was nothing they could do but wait. David was not expected to wake until the next day; if they were early, they could be with him as he came round. Joe asked Flora to stay with him, as her apartment was a mess. He gave her a key so she could come and go as she pleased. They both spent as much time as possible in the hospital, Joe even took time off work. After only a week David was allowed to leave the hospital, although it would be a long time before he could work again, as a model at least. Joe arranged to pick him up. The traffic was slow in the West End, and he had so much to do. He bought a cake, made especially, with little fat, from Maison Bertaux. In Piccadilly Circus he picked up a C.D, David's new favorite.

The list of chores seemed endless. Driving from the record shop he passed Flora's office, and decided to call in to see when she'd be finished. He got out of his car, ran up to the reception. But it was Saturday, no one was there; There was no telephone box in sight either. He spotted what looked like Flora's car. Getting closer, he saw some dry-cleaning hanging over one window, and a toy David had given her. There was some mail in the back and some drawing pads. Not wanting to waste any more time he scrawled, "Call and let me know when to expect you." He stuck the note under a wiper.

Joe kept busy, hence distracted. When not by David's bed, he went to films and shows, even the ones he heard were dreadful. He had lunches with people connected with work that weren't really necessary. As long as there was babble in his head, he could rest. Joe needed new memories, to block the ones of David abused and destroyed. There was so much dealing with to be done, but a lot of avoidance happening instead.

On the day David got out of hospital, Flora was busy with an important presentation. She and David were both going to stay at Joe's, for the time being. Delighted at the prospect of having David in his house, Joe bought flowers, even cooked a special meal. Flora was to join them after work. The three of them had become like a family. Recent events had a consolidating effect; so for now, they were hardly ever apart. It had been years since Joe had felt so at ease with other people.

'And not a minute too soon,' said David. 'You know when some people say they hate hospitals, well, I really hate them.'

'Not that I'm keen,' said Joe, opening the car door, 'But, get in and make it snappy.'

Complaining that it hurt to laugh, David climbed in. With the door locked, he closed his eyes and sighed.

'Burn some rubber Daddy Joe. Get me out of here.'

David was being rescued. Joe enjoyed his role, or any that allowed him to show he cared.

'It's so good to have you back Sonny.'

'You never had me before,' said David.

'No, not yet.' Joe kept a serious face as long as he could, then burst out laughing. 'I couldn't resist it.'

'Cheeky.'

'Okay. It's so good to have you. Doesn't sound quite right, does it?'

'How about it's good to see me.'

'Okay. It's good to see me,' said Joe.

'You're such an idiot today.'

'I'm just happy that you're coming home.'

Joe looked round, and his expression gave away too much.

'I guess it's not so good to see me?' said David.

'Don't be stupid. It would be good to see you if you were inside out. Well, as long as that's how you wanted to be.'

'Arr! That's nice, I think.'

On their return, Flora answered the door.

'I got out on time, after all. I thought rather than rush to the hospital and miss you, I'd come straight here. I let myself in. You don't mind do you Joe?'

'Of course not.'

'Give me a cuddle, but gently,' said David. 'I'm glad you weren't stuck in the office all night.'

'I didn't actually have to go to the office.'

Half-hearing what Flora said, Joe put away their jackets.

'You poor thing,' said David. 'Having to work on a Saturday.'

'You're the one who needs sympathy,' said Joe. 'And we're going to suffocate you. Right Flora?'

'Sounds good to me.'

'In that case, fetch me a drink,' said David.

'Certainly sir.'

Joe left the room and kitchen noises could be heard, then a long silence.

'Is everything okay?' shouted Flora.

Again, there was silence.

'Joe, are you alright?' Both David and Flora headed towards the kitchen. 'What's going on?'

Joe was kneeling on the floor struggling with a bag. Half in the bag was a parcel. He turned and stood up.

'Come on, let's sit down.'

Leading David into the living room, Joe turned towards Flora and winked conspiratorially.

'Make some tea, will you Flora? The water's boiled.'

CAUGHT

Joe tucked David in bed.
　'Where did you say you were going again?'
　'I didn't say.'
　'Okay where are you going?'
　'We're going for a drive.'
　'Oh, Flora's going with you?'
　'That's right. I'll tell you all about it later.'
　'I'll be asleep later.'
　'Exactly.'
　'I guess I'll have to wait then.'
For now David felt less like laughing, being loud, or doing battle. Only one of his eyes could open properly. The other, along with most of his face was still too bruised. If his mind were on the outside, he would look even shabbier. Joe kissed David's forehead, extra softly.
　'David, do you?'
　'No, never.'
　'Please don't joke for a minute.' The seriousness of Joe's tone quiets David.
　'When I met you, I was so attracted to you.'
　David's mind bolts.
　'This has changed.' Joe continued. 'Now, I just love you.'
　More panic. David began to sweat. He heard noises in the street and smelt a waft of dinner that was still in the air. Attaching to anything, his focus surfed - anything but Joe.
　'I love you as a friend.' Joe saw doubt and fear but knew David was just catching up. 'Honestly.' Smiling, Joe pretended to tickle him. 'I'm no monster,' he said, then contorted his face, almost beyond recognition. This distracted David long enough for him to lose his thoughts and go with the moment. 'I'm the fairest maiden in all the land. Won't you marry me?'
　David laughed. 'Okay, but only because I feel sorry for you.' They both laughed. 'Silly Bugger,' said David. Tears came to Joe's eyes. This made them laugh even more.
　'*Buggerer,* if you don't mind.'
　'Sorry. I didn't mean to offend. You know, they used to

get arrested for doing that.'

'That's only because *they* weren't doing it properly.'

'Oh really, and you know how to do it properly.'

'You bet.'

Flora came in.

'What's going on?'

'Nothing,' said David, as he poked Joe with his foot, through the blankets.

'Are we ready to leave?'

'We're ready,' said Joe. He kissed David on the side of his head and whispered. 'Trust me.'

They shared a good look, but David was tired and Joe was too preoccupied to enjoy it.

'Come on you,' said Flora as she took Joe's arm.

'Coming.'

'Sleep tight baby,' said Flora.

Sleep tight baby, thought Joe, as he left David to sleep; but also, took him along, storing him within.

THE DRIVE

Joe drives fast. He has his window wide open. The warm night air rushes into the car. It should have felt beautiful but, for Joe, it doesn't.

'The first time I met you, I couldn't decide,' Joe hesitates. 'Whether I was jealous of you, or if I was becoming infatuated with you both.'

'I thought you were odd.'

'Don't say that. The only odd thing was that I felt so bloody comfortable.'

Flora watches Joe. His jeans scrunch up on his thighs, emphasising his crotch. She thinks him very sexy. She's careful not to let him catch her looking.

'Where exactly are we going?' she asks.

'It's a secret.'

'I hope it's worth it.'

'Don't you trust me?' he says, looking at her. She melts.

'Keep your eyes on the road. Yes, of course I trust you. That's if we don't both get killed on the way.'

If things were different, if she were not with David, Joe would be so much what she wanted. On more than one occasion she had contemplated them all living together, or at least fucking together.

'Relax,' said Joe.

'These cliffs are dangerous.'

'Yes but it's worth it. The view is breathtaking. It's just a little farther.'

Rounding a bend, they pull into a stone pathway that takes them off the road. Winding, they bump and shake their way through a few trees. These open, to reveal a clifftop view of sky and sea. They stop and get out of the car.

'What now?' says Flora. 'It's beautiful and everything but...' She half expects he's going to make a move on her.

'Okay. We've got some talking to do.'

'So talk.' Flora thinks Joe is referring to her and he.

'It's miles to the nearest phone box, and quite a walk to the road. That's if there's any traffic on it.'

'So, what's your point?'

'My point is. You're not going anywhere until I get some answers.'
'You sound like a cop.'
'Whatever. I'm serious.'
'Have I been kidnapped?'
'I guess so.'
'You look serious.'
'I am.'
'What are you up to?'
'Sssh. Just listen Flora.'
'Are you mad?'
'No,' he shouts. 'It's you who's fucking mad.'
'Why are you so angry?'
'My God!' Joe can't believe his ears. 'You're fucked!'
'What are you talking about?'
'You hurt David.'
'I love him.'
'Yeah, and he loves you, because he doesn't know.'
'He doesn't know what?'
Joe slaps her. 'Don't play with me. Don't.'
'He's right to love me.'
'Stop. I know what you did.'
'What?'
'I saw the parcel in your fucking car.'
'Oh.'
'Is that all you can say?'
'Uhm.'
'Well, did you send them?'
Softly, 'Yes, I did.'
'Please explain?'
Pausing she looks away. Then she brings her eyes back to look at Joe, 'I wanted him to need me.'
'That must be the most pathetic thing I've ever heard.'
'Maybe, but it's the truth.'
'You didn't have to do this. He obviously loves you.'
'Joe, he's so beautiful. Things were changing. I saw him looking at others...at men. I even saw him looking at you.'
'And?'
'And I couldn't face that.'

'So you scare him half to death.'
'It worked, he's different now.'
'He's terrified and crushed. Is this how you wanted him?'
'I've got to have *something* of him.'
'Crazy bitch.'
'He still loves me, doesn't he?'
'Of course he does.'
'So.'
'So, you almost killed him.'
'What do you mean?'
'The attack,' says Joe.
'I had nothing to do with that.'
'What?'
'I don't know anything about that. I could never hurt him. You believe me, don't you?' Flora begins to cry. 'I'm not capable of that.'
'I don't know what to think,' says Joe.
They both stand looking at the ground. For over a minute they don't speak.
'What now?' says Joe.
'Are you going to tell him?'
'Of course I am,' but then he sees how pitiful she looks. 'I don't know.'
'Please don't. Please! He's everything to me.'
'You expect me to lie? '
'Please, Joe, he'd hate me.'
'Let me sleep on it.'
'Can we go home?' Flora is pure child now. Her face is wet and her mascara has smudged.
'I guess so, but I think it would be best if I took you back to your place.'
'Okay.'
Back in the car, it feels weird that they have to do something practical again, sit so close, share a journey, it's almost intimate. Not a word is said for several miles.
'Flora, what were you thinking? There must have been another way, don't you think?'
'Maybe. It all seems clear now. Before, it seemed like

there was no other way.'

'I know this is corny, but you need help. I'm serious.'

'I've already thought of that.'

Her head is down and she plays with her fingers. She opens the window, then closes it.

'I won't say anything tonight,' says Joe. 'I'll call you in the morning, we'll talk some more.'

'Thanks Joe. I couldn't have a better friend. I mean it.'

THE PARCEL

Flora answered the door. 'I got out on time, after all.' Joe's mind was on other things, but Flora's voice drifted in. '...I'd come straight here. You don't mind do you Joe?'

'Of course not.'

'I didn't actually have to go to the office.' That's not right, thought Joe.

'You poor thing,' said David.

'You're the one who needs sympathy,' said Joe. 'And we're going to suffocate you. Right Flora?' Joe looked at her and was confused, but didn't understand why. He went to the kitchen, so they could be alone. First, he put the kettle on. Then, he put away the groceries and took out what he needed for dinner. Next, he cleared off the counter top and threw away some over-ripe fruit. That was when he spotted the bag under the table. He crouched down and opened it.

'Are you alright in there?' shouted Flora from the living room. Joe was dead still. 'Is everything okay?' came Flora's voice again. There was a parcel in the bag. 'Joe are you alright?' Footsteps approached. Joe fumbled whilst trying to replace the bag. 'What's going on?' said Flora, as she and David entered the room. Joe got up and acted as though nothing had happened. Calmly, he put his arm around David's shoulder.

'Come on, let's sit down. Make some tea will you Flora, the water's boiled.'

Realising that something odd had happened David glanced around the room. Joe hadn't managed to conceal the bag very well. David saw it. 'Where did that come from?' he asked. David's shock was only outweighed by his confusion.

'I put it there,' said Flora. 'I'm sorry if it shocked you, baby. I collected it from the house this evening. I wasn't sure whether to tell you.'

'It's nice of you to protect me, but...' This was too soon for David. 'I just don't understand. Why's this still happening?' David started to snivel. 'Didn't he get what he wanted?'

As often happened lately, Joe's thoughts scattered. Why did Flora say she hadn't gone to the office? Then other thoughts wrenched his stomach. The car today. Flora's car. The mail. The mail had a parcel with it. Today, not this evening. Flora had the parcel today. His thoughts stuck as though damaged. If this were real, then he was faulty. Rather this, than to realise what might have gone on and why? How could Joe find out the truth?

'Lets not deal with it now,' said David. 'Not tonight.' He looked tired.

'Shall I just put it in the bin?' said Joe.

'No.' Flora replied quickly. 'We've got to get this sorted out.'

'Okay,' said Joe, 'But, in the morning.'

Barely holding the evening together, Joe put on a video; at least he wouldn't have to make conversation. This gave him a couple of hours to decide what to do, but it wasn't enough. There was no peace in sleep for Joe, so he had even longer to think everything over. In more detail than before, he saw evil had a face. It still had the hands and will of evil; but now it smiled, talked, and kissed his forehead. It joined him for lunch, and hugged him good night. It lied and lied and fucked his David. All the time knowing something else, knowing the truth which was about untruth. He loathed her. How he wished he could have seen it sooner, before so much damage had been done, but it was too far from honesty to recognise. Flora's was another place, with another language. Joe would have to decipher her contorted jargon, listen for her confession, set a trap to reveal what was hidden.

Finally it was morning and he could stop trying to sleep. A secret mission took him out of the house, returning just in time to fix breakfast and wake up the others.

'Good morning my little prince,' he said, 'Eggs okay?'

'If that's the smell that got me out of bed, I'd love some.'

Many things were unsaid over breakfast. When there was so much to avoid, very little was left to discuss. Chewing and slurping. Crunching and swallowing. These sounds became a joke. David made a sound effect like he was eating a rock.

'Hush!' Joe said. 'I can't hear ourselves talk.'
Flora looked baffled.
'Well, you're not saying anything,' said Joe in response.
'I just feel so bad about bringing in that parcel last night.'
Now it was out in the open. It had only been a matter of coughs and clinks before it reared itself.
'I've been thinking,' Joe announced. 'We really should open it. Don't ask me why, but I think we should all the same.'
'I think it's up to David,' said Flora.
'What's the point?' answered David in a weak voice.
Joe was keen. 'There is no point. But I for one would have a hard time just throwing it in the bin.'
'There is that option,' Flora adds.
Joe headed towards the drawer to get a pair of scissors, 'I say open it.'
'No Joe.' David hesitated, but Joe gave him a look that seemed to say it was fine. 'Are you sure about this?'
'Yes,' said Joe, wanting to hold David, kiss him, and let him know things were under control now.
Meticulously Joe snipped at the box, as though it were a gift. He put his hand in, barely looking, not worried what he might find.
A beautiful rose appeared. As fast as a camera shutter, Joe caught Flora's response, delicate but definite: confusion and anger, until she managed a coerced smile. Flora didn't notice him watching, she was far too surprised. David's response was lost as noise: a gasp, then squeals.
'What's going on?' he said.
'I don't know,' said Joe. 'But there's a note inside.'
'What does it say? Joe what does it say?'
'It says, "I love you sweet man," and it's signed with a J. Who can that be?'
'Joe, but how?'
'I changed it this morning. I wanted to surprise you. I did didn't I?'
Then to Flora, 'Didn't I?'

TRUTH

Flora let herself in. She crept up to the room where David was. Quietly, she opened the door, pulling it just less than she pushed it, to make sure it didn't squeak. Her footsteps were soft, she wore sneakers especially. Even asleep, David looked troubled. Maybe he was having a bad dream, or maybe he had brought his bad reality into his sleep.

Flora put her hand on his shoulder and coaxed him awake. If he jolted, he might make too much noise. Gently she rocked him.

'Baby, wake up.' She spoke in a whisper, barely audible. 'Baby, it's me, Flora.'

The doctor had prescribed David Rohypnol, to help him sleep. It was difficult to wake him. As David didn't respond, Flora used more might. David began to wake. 'Baby, it's me. Baby. It's Flora.' David was so out of it he wasn't shocked to see her. Flora tried to get him to sit up, but couldn't, he was floppy. 'Come on baby, wake up.' She shook him hard.

'Ow,' said David. 'What do you want?'

'We've got to get out of here, baby. We've got to go home.'

'What do you mean. I was asleep.'

'I know baby, but something real bad has happened. We've got to go home.'

'I don't want to. Can't it wait.'

Flora had been pushed too far. She slapped David hard. 'What the fuck?'

'I'm serious, you've got to wake up.'

'There's no need for that.' He was confused.

'I'm sorry baby. But, we've got to leave.'

'What about Joe? Where is he?'

'I can't explain yet. Wait until we're in the car.'

'Is he coming?'

'No. We have to get away from him.'

David was completely baffled. He clumsily got dressed. Flora rallied around the room, collecting his stuff.

'Tell me what's going on,' said David, too loudly.

'Sssh. I'm not kidding. Just get what you need, leave the rest.'

'Are we coming back?'

'Not if I have anything to do with it.'

'I don't understand.'

'You don't have to, I'll explain in the car I promise.'

David stuffed things into his bag. 'Leave anything that's not important.' Flora's urgency worried David. He felt upset, dragged out of sleep, confronted with yet more weirdness. 'Leave your shoes off, we've got to be quiet.'

David did as he was told and they slipped out of the house. At the front door David tried to pull on his shoes, but was stopped. 'Quickly into the car.' The ground was wet, within a few steps it soaked through his socks.

'Ugh! Flora.'

'Come on.'

They got in the car and without a pause, the key was turned and they were off.

'Can you please tell me what that was all about?' Flora was silent, she stared ahead. 'Hello! Flora. What's going on?'

Without turning to look at him, without blinking, she said. 'Joe sent the parcels.'

For the rest of the journey Flora thrashed out the finishing touches to her story.

David got out of the car, and as though he had no soul, was led into Flora's apartment, their home.

Flora explained that she had seen scraps of paper in the garbage can outside the house. They were the same as the paper used on the parcels. This, was after the second one had been sent. She also had found a marker on Joe's desk, the same thickness and colour as was used on the parcels.

'I can hardly tell you the rest,' said Flora. 'It's so creepy.'

'What?'

'He took me out in the car. And I was being friendly. But he started acting all sleazy, started coming on to me.'

David thought for a second of what Joe had said. Trust me. Maybe, Joe had been trying to manipulate him, turning him against Flora. Could Flora be lying?

'I don't believe it,' said David.

'Well it's true, he started telling me what he'd like to do to us.'

'What, both of us?'

'Yes, he said that he wanted a three-way, and could I swing it. Those were his words. Ugh, it makes me shiver thinking about it.'

'What did you say?'

'I didn't know what to say. I was a bit scared. I thought, If he can turn like this, keep secrets, make friends with us, and yet have something else on his mind all the time, it doesn't bear thinking about what he might be capable of.'

'Jesus Christ!'

'He made me promise not to say anything. I can't even repeat some of the stuff he said.'

'He probably thought you were into it.'

'I think he did. He said...' Flora stopped.

'What? You've got to tell me.'

'He said he'd like to...' Again, she stopped.

'Please Flora. It's probably better to say it. Don't keep it in.'

'He said he'd like to eat my cunt and...' Flora looked down as though she were ashamed that the words were coming out of her mouth.

'And what Flora?'

'And "eat your sweet arse," then fuck us both, "when we were hot and ready for it."'

In the morning Joe woke up to find David gone, the house empty. There was no note. He called Flora. There was no answer. Not that morning, afternoon, evening, or any following. Joe went round to the apartment. There was no one there. David and Flora had collected some stuff and left that morning for a two-week holiday, which stretched out for several months. Flora had wanted a big break and this seemed as good a time as any. Whilst away they'd have their telephone number changed, they'd have fun together, fall back in love and stay together, this was Flora's plan. Whilst in Spain, away from gossip, oppression, and London everydayness, David sucked the dick of a soldier who filled his mouth and belly with cum. Christmas came and although David had made a promise to Ryan, he was persuaded to fly with Flora to Orlando instead. They spent two days at Disney World, minutes of which David spent in the men's toilets on his knees. Flora was pleased to see him look happy again. For David the future seemed clearer with each encounter.

Joe went to their house repeatedly. The first week he called round everyday. He couldn't see any lights on in their apartment, so by the second week he assumed they were not there. Sometime during the third week he left a letter, simply saying, please call. He tried David's agency and even Flora's work place, but couldn't get hold of either of them. A month passed and Joe tried to face up to the reality that he probably wouldn't see David again. It all seemed so dramatic. One minute David was there, the next, nothing. Joe toyed with the idea of going to the police, but it was so complex. They'd probably think he was some crazed serial-homo. He couldn't face that.

BREAKAWAY

London seemed grim after warm nights, sea air and freedom. Everything had a second hand feeling to it, musky, worn out, rotting.

'Shall we get the tube?' said Flora.

'No, I'm really tired.'

'You sound like an old man.'

'You sound angry.'

It wasn't that Flora sounded angry, but there was an ugly force to her words. Her lips curled to a sharp angle as though they had something nasty on them, or maybe the lips themselves wanted to be away from, cease to be, the mouth she ordinarily kissed with.

David couldn't stay. Repelled, David started to run.

'What are you doing!' Her confusion cried, "David!"

'Leave me alone,' he shouted and continued to run. After only a short distance he slowed to a jog. David checked. He wasn't being followed, so slowed to a walking pace. He passed people being friendly at each other, so quickened again. The last thing he needed was a reminder that others got it right. He realised he'd gone in the wrong direction, so started to double back. He went down a ramp that led to street level. Now he had time to think, but still no time to feel. So he continued into the taxi-less, people-less, under-construction jumble of broken walkways behind the National Theatre.

'David! David! David!' shouted Flora from the bridge over head. This was the starting pistol, to run again. She looked tiny, and even more confused. Something lifted David from within and drove him forward. For seconds he felt glorious and free, running in the night, strong and energized. Then it happened. He felt guilt. David envisioned a woman having to run after her lover, lost and not knowing, twisted from normal and so far away from their sweet-eating, meal making, blissful in loveness of before.

Consumed with how Flora might feel, David stopped, turned, sat on a wall and watched her running towards him. As she got closer, David gestured her to sit beside him. She clambered onto the wall, sulking. She accepted the hand that started to stroke her neck. David did this to show affection, mixing his uncertain message further.

'What's going on?'
'I stopped because I don't want you to be upset.'
Flora looked confused.
'Why did you run away?' she said.
'Because you sounded angry.'
'I didn't... It was a joke.'
'It sounded angry to me.'
'It was a joke...It was just a joke.'

All David could see was hurt. So he jumped down off the wall, in an attempt to punctuate the situation. They walked with their heads down, as though looking for answers in the flagstones. The South Bank had never looked so romantic, and the Thames, never so frigid. It was a clear evening, bright and calm. David wanted to try and reset Flora's upset heart. 'Do you know what's going on?'

'No!' There was an urgency to everything Flora said. Her voice seemed to resonate with a quality David hadn't heard from her before. It came from a different place than usual, her chest, or just a little farther down her throat. Somewhere one step removed from her vocal chords, somewhere David didn't know. This was unsettling. He had caused this, and felt responsible.

'I don't think we can go on the way we have been.'
'What are you saying?'
'I'm happy with you, but, I think this happiness isn't the right thing for me. Do you understand?'
'No.'
'I don't know if I do.'
'Is it about Joe?'
'No. Well, maybe.'
'What?'
'Something about who, or what I am.'
'What are you talking about?'
'Let's leave it.'

'No. You can't just tell me it's over and then say, "let's leave it."'

'I didn't say it's over.'

'Yes you did.'

'I didn't. Don't you understand?'

'Should I?'

'I think you knew how I felt, didn't you?' Flora was silent. 'Didn't you?'

After a long pause, 'I think I did.' She paused again, then without looking at David she said, 'So. What now?'

'I'm not sure. Something to do with just being me.'

'But. I still feel the same. I still want you.'

'Do you think for a second that I've stopped loving you? Do you?'

'No. I guess not.'

'We've got to change.'

'It sounds like the end.'

'It's the end of one thing, that's all. Not even the end, just a change.'

By this point, the couple were halfway across Westminster Bridge, heading towards the Houses of Parliament. They were closed off to traffic, which made Big Ben look isolated and its surrounds desolate.

David thought he had been too aggressive. 'Give me a hug?' he said.

'Okay,' said Flora with a blank expression and still that displaced voice. David lost himself in her neck for a short time, until his guarded-self took hold again.

'I need time to think. You go home. I'll follow you shortly.'

Flora got in a cab. David walked off in the direction of Soho realising it was time to live by himself.

ALONE

Life can get dull with no one to love, or like, or even to touch. What David missed the most was someone always being around. There were many things he had become accustomed to, from teeth brushing noises each morning, to somebody else's movements in bed at night.

Flora had cared so much. David wondered how he could have given that up. In the back of his mind, David had some trouble believing the truth about Joe. Could anyone be that obsessive, calculating and false? David was thankful that Flora was there when he needed her, to work it all out.

David had contracted H.I.V. when he was raped. It was something he had feared, but had put to the back of his mind. When trying to live a new life, on his own, he had got the courage together to go for a test. A nurse gave him a look of concern. Then he was handed over to a counsellor who explained what she knew; a strange mix of deep routed morality, yet, very little information about the virus. In what was becoming his usual state, confused, he left the hospital. He drove through the West End, it was the same as it had been on the way. Looking out of the windscreen, the weather was the same as before. Yet, everything seemed different. Lights and people seemed distanced, removed by his experience. He felt alone, with no one he cared to turn to.

'Everything's okay. I'll deal with this. I've got money saved. I'm strong. I'm young. I'll be fine.' Underneath these thoughts was another: 'I'm going to die.' This was the strongest thought of all. It could easily drag him down to a depth where he saw nothing.

That evening whilst sitting in his still empty apartment, he cried. There was no warning. It was in, then flowing freely. Since becoming an adult, he had not done this. Not after the news of Joe, or when he left Flora, not since he was very young. The handkerchief he was using became completely wet, then so did his sleeve. All of his face, his hands, his hair, everything got wet. These tears were real, the kind it's not practical to indulge in all the time but, on special occasions, they were just the thing.

After several days and nights he took a shower, shaved, made coffee, reinstated himself in his life.

All this pulling together and getting on was for a special reason. After viewing this new life, he decided he didn't want to be alone. So the priority became, finding a companion, a man. David wanted to love someone again. Not anyone, the one, his one. He would love everything about them. In return, they must love only him, every part of him, - the part who might die, and the part who was terrified of this.

SHOPPING

In the supermarket, a man came up behind David, next in line at the checkout. They had met about five years ago. The man was still attractive, he'd always had such a fresh look about him. David had spotted him here, reading at the magazine counter, earlier in the week. Then before that, in a cafe a few months ago.

'Hi.' David felt nervous.

'Hi,' said the man with a wink.

'Long time no see.'

David felt, the man wanted him to carry on the conversation. David wanted to.

'Yeah.'

'I saw you here the other day, reading the magazines.'

'Yeah, I do that a lot. I work next door.' His complexion looked like he'd come straight from the playground. 'You know, in the cinema.'

'That's my local. I live just round the corner.'

David was distracted by the checkout woman. She seemed bored and looked at though she were permanently stifling a yawn. David was asked to take his shopping out of the basket. There were two main responses given by the assistants. One, unconvincingly friendly. The other, barely offering enough communication to complete the task. The assistant looked impatient, whilst David packed his shopping. He juggled his attention from person to person, the checkout's annoyance with his friend's inviting facial expressions. David dealt with the money and started to pack his groceries.

'I only came to get a sandwich,' the man said holding it up to show David. He paid with the correct change so they both finished at the same time.

David tried to catch the eye of the checkout woman saying, 'Thanks very much.' Trying to be as genuine as he could.

On the way to the shop David had seen the Saturday bustle and felt a great deal. There were people in shops looking at objects. In one, a boy holding a birthday card.

David hoped that it was for somebody who made the boy happy.

Moving down the street a little, to the end of the same shop. David caught sight of an older man, maybe a husband, holding a pink triangular bottle. David guessed it was bubblebath. His cynicism took hold of him, watching the man turning the object in his hand, confused by it's femaleness. The man continued turning it, looking possibly for a label, any kind of answer to the question, Will it do? David imagined a family scene. A wife opening her present, smiling and loving her husband for being so thoughtful, putting energy into her gift, into her. It being a symbol of his love, of all the good things in their relationship.

Now David stood outside the cinema with the man from the supermarket.

'You can come and see this if you like,' the man said, pointing to the poster for a film.

'I've seen it.'

'Did you like it?'

'I don't know.'

'It's coming off early. It's not doing so well.'

David moved his groceries from hand to hand, then over one shoulder. Should he rest his arms by putting the bags on the pavement? Would this look too much like he wanted to stay with the man longer?

'Woody Allen's new one is on next.'

'I'll give it a miss.'

'I can get comps.'

'Oh, alright. I'll watch anything.'

'Just ask for me.'

'I'll take you up on that.'

'I'm always here. Well it feels like it. Most evenings anyway.'

'Great. I mean, great for me.'

'Thanks.'

There was silence and, for the first time, it felt okay.

'Weren't you involved in music or something?' said David, forcing his memory.

'No, design.'

'That's right, really it was so long ago. Do you still do any?'

'Some. Yeah, now and then. I made some postcards,' said the man, with a hint of apology.

'Could I have one?'

'They're quite simple.'

'Even better. I'd love one.' David grinned and felt himself flirting, so, for some reason stopped.

'I don't even know if they'll make it through the post.'

'Deliver it then. I live just behind the church here.'

'I guess I could.'

'If you ring my doorbell, I'll make you a cup of tea. Shall I give you my address and number?'

The man accepted and gave David his number. Maybe this could go further. They had both grown older and presumably, both learnt about disappointment.

'You know, I didn't recognise you,' said the man. 'You've changed.'

'Same, same.'

'Who was that woman, I used to see you with.'

'My girlfriend.'

'Are you still seeing her?'

'No.'

'Is that a recent thing?'

'Yeah,' said David.

The man pulled off his baseball cap and rubbed his head. He had short-curly-stuck-to-his-head hair, got-up-not-combed-and-hid-under-a-cap hair. 'You look like you've just been born,' said David.

The man burst out laughing. 'Thanks, I think.'

'It *was* a compliment.'

Then, it was over. They had spent long enough together already and were both aware of it.

'It's been nice talking to you,' said the man. David never saw him again.

CONNECTION

Whilst reading through the personals in a gay paper, David noticed an ad. It was clearer than the rest, somehow understated, only a few lines in length. As much as he wanted to, David wouldn't reply. It seemed too sad to resort to ads.

David spent an awful day hanging around Thermos sauna. Then he spent an equally miserable evening in coffee shops and bars. Each time he went into his pocket to get at some change, out came the ad. Finally he gave in and wrote a letter. In it he was much too honest.

A photograph had to be sent with the letter. David didn't want to use a professional one, it might come across as pretentious, and anyway he felt these didn't represent him anymore. He searched, but could only find pictures of Flora and him in Greece, Flora and him in Spain, in Vancouver and Seattle. There was a cute one and one of Donald Duck and himself, but not one on his own. None of these seemed appropriate, so he sent a booth photo instead.

It was a short letter, but a lot was read from it. A couple of weeks later David received a reply. It was even shorter. Enclosed were a photo, as incentive, and a note which read, 'Dear David, phone me, I'd like to meet you. Rob.'

Rob had, in fact, wanted to say much more, about his own life, and, how endearing he found David's photo. But, he didn't, he was careful.

David thought the note curt, but thought Rob looked sexy. He left the photo on the sideboard and glanced at it throughout the day. The face became familiar to him, warm and even responsive. David decided to call.

'Hello is that Rob?'
'No, he's not here. Can I take a message?'
'Can you just tell him David called?'
'Sure thing, has he got your number?'
'No.'
'Go ahead then I've got a pen.'
Before David had time to consider, the number came

out. He wished he hadn't, then he was glad he had, then he wished he hadn't; this continued throughout the day. Who'd answered the phone anyway? Was it a lover or someone else Rob had already met.

Later that evening, the telephone rang and the right kind of voice asked for David. They talked for a while, then Rob suggested they meet somewhere for lunch. David suggested a restaurant thinking he would get there first, in order to prepare for the arrival of his date. Rushing to do this, he got the tube to avoid busy traffic. Distracted, he caught the wrong one and ended up stressed. As he neared his destination, it started to rain heavily. By the time he arrived, he felt shitty, all dripping hair and sticking clothes.

'David?'

'Rob.'

There was no magical spark between these men. They'd had different experiences, but they wanted the same thing. So they listened and responded, awkward sometimes and sometimes not. They looked at each other and saw much. Both of them were definite about what they had become, but unsure of their worth. When they parted, hours later, both were sure of something. They would do this again, and soon.

CHRISTMAS

Joe was out of David's life, but not out of his mind. Something of Joe lingered, if not, at least a desire to talk to him, to try and find out why he had been so cruel.

After being let down, last year, Ryan was really looking forward to his Christmas visit. David called Judy to check the details.

'You're still coming, aren't you?' said David.

'Of course. I've still so many presents to get. I can leave the special things until then.'

David had been keeping an eye open for a present for Ryan. At eight years old, Ryan was getting too old for some toys, so David thought about getting him a book. Around this time of year the newspaper had a review of all the best books for children. Some of them sounded too educational, or too lightweight. There was one entitled *Star*, David's mind flashed back to the conversation with Joe. "You're a shining star." The review read;

Written by the inexhaustible Joseph Holtzman, we are taken on a journey of a child on a wish. This tale expresses Holtzman's love of the visual, with vivid descriptions of imaginary happenings. Its use of language may be difficult for younger children. Explanations may be necessary, but not for this alone. Holtzman takes for granted a male-to-male partnership, which he handles so comfortably, your child may not know they're meant to find it "pretend," or unusual. This is a story of love and magic, so all is accepted and expected. Charming, of the old school, but with a postmodern twist. Read yourself first. You might find it strangely engaging.

Books etc, on Charing Cross Road, was David's first stop of the day. He asked for Joe's book. The cover was made of an iridescent, reflective material. When moved at different angles to the light, it changed colour. It was a handsome book, something that a child would probably treasure. David opened it and read
Dedicated
to

David Michael

David mouthed, 'Joe.' With this word, he meant: I don't understand. And many thoughts less structured, more felt. David stood and read the whole story in the shop; then with a mixture of pride and a touch of embarrassment, paid for it and went to work. After having had so much time off, whilst out of the country, David realised he was unhappy modeling. Tentatively, he got a job in a gym, working six evenings a week. At least he could get away with simply looking sporty. He knew his way around the equipment well enough to appear convincing. It wasn't a gay gym, but David felt as though the men looked at him as much as the women. He switched off to this at work.

On the nineteenth of December David picked up Judy and Ryan. He was thankful the rest of the family didn't want to come. First, he dropped off their stuff, then headed for the West End. David asked Judy if he could read Joe's story to Ryan. 'I suppose it can't do him any harm,' she said. Then thinking for a second she continued, 'But he'll have questions, and believe me they can be really difficult.' David thought this was more about Judy than Ryan, and wasn't worried. Whilst shopping, trekking past grotesque Christmas displays, they stopped for a coffee.

'Where's your girlfriend?' asked Ryan.

'I don't have one anymore,' said David.

'Are you going to get another?'

'No.' David stared into his coffee. 'I don't think so.'

'Why not?'

David looked at Judy for assurance.

'Yeah why not?' said Judy, who knew exactly why already.

'I don't want to.'

'Why?' said Ryan.

'I'm not into girls.'

Ryan laughed. 'Are you into boys?'

'I don't know.'

'You can't have a boyfriend,' said Ryan.

'Okay, manfriend.'

Judy rolled her eyes. Ryan didn't miss a beat. 'Idiot. You

can't have a manfriend?'

'You can,' said David. 'I think.' Turning to Judy he said, 'This coffee's good.'

'Yeah. Nice.'

Judy gave no clue as to how this situation should be handled, but just looked ahead and sipped her coffee.

'Can I have a manfriend?' asked Ryan.

David was speechless.

'Maybe when you're older dear,' said Judy and winked at David. This seemed to suffice, and Ryan became engrossed in sucking up the cream from his hot chocolate.

When home David and Ryan watched corny Christmas shows and relaxed. Judy was out visiting an old school friend.

'Can you have a manfriend?' asked Ryan, as though still in mid-conversation.

'I hope so,' said David.

Ryan pointed at something on the television and laughed. He snuggled into David's side, basking in his attention, unselfconsciously. Rolling his head on David's lap, he smiled, showing his peggy teeth.

'Watch this, watch this,' Ryan said, then acted as though he was dead, but with exaggerated, staring eyes. David stuck his finger in Ryan's ear, tickling him. Ryan came alive with a screech. This kind of play went on all evening, until it was time for bed.

'You go up and get in. I've got a story to read to you.'

'Fantastic!' Ryan said, which David thought very Seventies, but assumed it must have come around again. Running upstairs, he shouted "Fantastic!" again.

David cleared up a little, then followed Ryan.

'It's called *Star*.' David said in his best storybook, uncle's voice. He began to read as Ryan snuggled into his pillow, surrounding himself with cotton softness.

'"There was once a girl, who wished that she could sing. At school, she dared not open her mouth, dreading what might come out. But, every night, at bedtime, with no one around to make her feel her voice was ugly, she would practice. Her room was painted in many different colours.

Her father was a decorator, so was often left with odd pots of paint. He was able to create something, which, like all the colours in a summer garden, didn't annoy. He had a sensitive eye, and his girl a sensitive soul. The kind of soul that can feel at one with a squirrel hopping around the frozen pathways in the depth of winter. The kind that others seem to take pleasure in crushing. This soul could be seen as an ignition from which the whole world could catch fire or a single tear might put out. Souls like this must be looked after because they have a habit of throwing themselves into things with too much bravery."'

David turned to Ryan and made a mad, overly smiley face. In response, a miniature version tried to do the same thing. But the muscles in Ryan's face couldn't hold it for long. It broke down into a more beautiful, real smile.

'Do you want me to carry on?'

'Yeah it's fantastic.' David thought this sounded forced and imagined Ryan's friends using the same word at school. Then, remembering he really didn't have a clue how children thought, or most adults, he carried on.

'"This was a night early in spring. And the crocus in its mud bed stirred with anticipation. The sky outside grew darker, and the colours in the room began to fade. They slid out of sight until only tones were left. Even these seemed cleverly arranged as though planned. The girl sat by her window and sang. The moon shone down, dusting her face with white. For some reason, she began to lower her head, giving her the look of a snowdrop. A tear clung so heavy on her chin that her face might have lifted when it fell. But it didn't."'

'That's dramatic,' interrupted Ryan.

'Settle down you,' said David. Then he sighed. How sweet Ryan looked with his bedclothes pulled up high and his fingers peeping out from underneath his chin. He seemed to possess that strange mix of innocence and coquettishness that Disney characters do.

In a classroom fourteen or fifteen years before, during religious education, David had learned many things. The teacher was peculiar to look at. The kind, in retrospect, you wonder how they ever fitted into normal society. Her hair, her skirt, those shoes and that completely eccentric, but very normal, manner. This teacher caught David watching her. Splitting some part of him open she managed to trample into him. To a more mature, little David, she said, 'Don't flutter your eyelashes at me young man.' David had not wanted to be dragged into adulthood, but he'd had no choice. Within a second, and for only a short time, he had to deal with an adult girl. Someone who had created a place where they might lie down together, might take off their clothes, and he might explore her body, her secret parts, the smells and taste and sounds of the parts that rested beneath her polyester skirt, the nylon of her tights and the gusset beyond. Had David been raped in this not so uncommon way? Had he been abducted with feet kicking into another, more horrific world? Had Mrs Burt seen inside, through the movement of his eyelids, seen the space which was to become his sexual self? Or had she seen what she wanted to see, someone, or something, anything that focused on her cunt?

Looking at Ryan, David smiled. He did not see from the outside, through the window of their room, this glowing scene of warmth. Nor could he see from inside the mind of a boy, who had all the admiration in the world for his uncle. Could this boy have understood the feelings this man had for him? This young open heart was at an advantage, for he didn't know what he was and was not meant to feel, or whom and whom not he was meant to feel it for. So he felt it, and it was cozy, and honest and sexual.

'"There came a sound, very faint, but clear."' David continued reading. '"It seemed to be coming from the moonlight. A rustling of music trickled into her room. A white melodic tinkling began to surround her. The room began to fill with this noise, although as it filled it did not get any louder. Stars came flickering into her room. She reached to touch one and a tickle washed over her fingers. Squeaking a giggle like a bicycle bell, she grabbed hold of one. Holding it close to her belly, she stooped over it. As she opened her fingers to peep in, starlight showered through. Climbing off her stool she ran over and up onto her bed. Behind her, she left a trail of shining stardust. Jumping up and down, she spun making a wall of shimmer which fell flickering around her. In her excitement she popped the star into her mouth, fell off her bed with a crash, then, gulping she swallowed it."'

'Oh my God,' Ryan said and put his hand to his mouth. David couldn't tell if he was joking, or if he was really wrapped up in the story.

'Oh my God what?' said David.

'She swallowed the star.'

'And?'

'And then what happened?'

'"Screeching bed springs began to quiet and all became still. Then she coughed and the noise of air that came from her mouth sounded so beautiful. It was so clear it seemed to have edges, but so soft that it had no end. Along with the sound came glittering sparkle. Her whole body was fit to split with excitement. She could not believe her own thoughts. Managing to scramble together the idea of what to do next she concentrated as pure as she could. From the deepest part of her tummy the little girl tugged at a note. Plucking it, she pulled it, shaped it and pushed it up towards her mouth. It scurried through her shivering lips and out blazed a sound that was perfect.

'"All the glistening in all the room had settled before she stirred again. Down the front of her vest and on her knees was a thin coating of iridescence. Lifting up her hand, she blew. Again from within her mouth a sound came glowing. It was like the whisper of a mother loving you to sleep, or the first real gust of spring speckled with every living smell. She put her hand over her mouth and lay down. She felt sapped of all excitement.

'"The light in the room was perfectly still until early morning. The shadow of the stool contorted slowly as the sun rose. Having tipped the bed hours before, now it became a pit by the window.

'"Time to wake up, sleepyhead,' came a voice from downstairs.

'"It was true there was a sleepyhead lying in bed today. A pair of sticky eyes opened. Then in a light, almost floating motion the little girl rose out of bed. Standing up she felt a little strange. She began to walk towards the door, then stopped. Something was different. Taking a few more steps she realised that she could not hear her own footsteps. Jumping off the floor she found herself rising higher than normal. When she landed all she could hear was the rattle of bowls and cutlery from downstairs. Remembering her father's call, she made her way downstairs for breakfast.

""Princess, I didn't hear you come in," said her father. The girl made no reply, only smiled.

""I've made you some porridge.

'"Whilst eating, she carefully slid the spoon in between her lips for fear some twinkling might escape. Her father noticed that there was something wrong.

""Why won't you open your mouth?" Of course the quiet girl dared not say a word.

""Is this some kind of game?

'"Again she could not answer. Barely managing to hide her bewilderment she gave him a very odd expression.

'Now it was obvious something was going on.

'"Are you alright? her father asked, getting slightly worried. There was no way out this time so she opened her mouth. To her surprise no sound came out, for she was still breathing through her nose. Whew, she thought. Then as soon as she started to reply to her father, a glimmer of morning harmony chased around the room. Fresher than the brightest reflections on water, no matter how much in love you are. This was something neither of them had heard before. Her father's eyes filled with tears. He reached out for his daughter and pulled her tight to his chest. There they stayed, a slowly heaving chest and a squashed up pretty face.

""What has happened to you?

'"The girl tried her best to answer. The problem was as she started to speak she lifted from her seat. Like a dandelion clock she floated, coating the room with sugary sparkle.

'"Far away, in a cottage concealed by trees. A man was standing in his garden throwing ground spice into the wind. Like the little girl, this man also had a wish, but he was losing faith. The day before, an old woman had come knocking on his door. She'd asked for the handsomeness from his face, and in return she would make his wish come true. So deep was his desire for this, he'd willingly given her what she wanted.

'"He would never be called handsome again, but within him he still had beauty. He cared as he always had, carried himself as he always had, and tried to understand as he always had. This man's beauty shone from an intensely rich core. Kneeling in his garden, he cried. He felt he understood nothing. After all, he was an adult, so was use to structuring his thoughts and using solid words to describe them. What good could he possibly be doing wishing in the wind? Feeling confused and tricked, he went back into his house."'

David looked over to Ryan, whose lids twitched sleepily. Then, he flicked open his eyes.

'I'm not asleep.'

'I know that.'

'So what happens next.'

'Shall I finish it tomorrow?'

'No stay.'

'Okay, I'll finish it. But it's really no problem if you fall asleep.'

'I bet I don't.'

'"How could he have known that a little girl in a different place was having the most unusual time. Now squashed against the ceiling, she sobbed. Her father could not bear to hear this. The walls were now coated with fishlike scales, thrashing rainbow rays from window to floor. He had to open the door to let his almost star-girl float out into the sky. As he stood in the frosty archway he simply cried and cried, seeing the most precious thing in his life slip away. He shouted as loud as he could. 'I love you!' This was clear, strong and pure like all things that come from the soul. It bellowed through the breeze, sounding more beautiful than anything the star-girl had heard before.

'"Rising and falling within air pockets, she bobbed along, now more star than girl. A sprinkle of spice rolled up her sparkly nose as she span, causing this glistening star-thing to sneeze. The force of which propelled her downwards, knocking her out of the sky. Falling and then falling farther, eventually she landed. A man who couldn't believe his tear tired eyes found her lying outside his door. He bent down to help her and as he did she floated up into his arms. Now, neither a girl nor a star, she was simply love. There was a moment then when everything stopped. A memory, a warmth, so familiar, so everlasting. This gift had been taken away. What separation could keep a child and a father from fitting together like the mouth of a clam, so tight and all protecting? Crying, it began to rain now. In the garden, everything from around them seemed to change. This spread outwards like a slow-motion explosion of good, through the grass, over early daffodils, in and out of thick woody ups and downs. As they lifted into the watery air it cradled their journey. Fast or slow, this journey took its own time, and when it ended, there was a man still looking into the sky. A man who had been waiting so long for what he saw. The sun's rays shrank his eyes and the rain freckled his face. Through layers of red, orange, yellow, green, blue, indigo then violet gently tumbled the little girl and the man whom they loved."'

David was absorbed. Focusing beyond the page, he stared into the past. He closed the book tenderly. It was a part of Joe. From his slouch, David looked up. Ryan was asleep. His soft face, so at peace. David hovered his lips over his nephew's head and smelt his gorgeous smell. Then he kissed him on the nose. Ryan woke up.

'Dave, will you sleep here?'
'What? You want to swap beds?'
'No, I want to sleep with you.'
David's stomach fluttered.
'No, you stay here and go to sleep.'
'Why can't I sleep with you?'

'Why would you want to?' said David.
'Because I like you.'
'No. I'm sorry.'
'Please.'
But I'll want to kiss you and squeeze you, thought David.
'Please, please, please, please, please, please.'
'Alright.'
Preparing for bed, thoughts began to tumble in his conscious mind. David was risking a lot by sleeping with the boy, but still he was keen to get into bed. He stripped to his boxer shorts. Switching off the light, he climbed in behind Ryan, who squashed his little bum up against him. Not content with this, Ryan turned around and clambered onto David's chest. He squirmed so much, David could feel his soft skin now, as the pajamas rose up his torso.

Predictably, David felt a pulse, then a throb start to grind inside his balls. No, deeper than his balls, behind them, inside. Knowing this would develop into a stiffened, sticking-out maybe strange-for-Ryan hard-on, he rolled over onto his front.

'Arh,' David feigned a yawn. 'I'm so tired. Goodnight Ryan.'

'Night, Dave. Night, Star-Girl.'

They both laughed and then settled. The hard-on melted into the softness of the mattress, and they into the sponginess of sleep.

David was awakened by the close of the front door. Judy was home. Fear shot through David. He jumped out of bed, into the bathroom and pretended he was brushing his teeth.

'David?'

'One minute.' He came out of the bathroom.

'Ryan asleep?' she said.

'Yeah, he went to bed ages ago.'

'Oh good.' She peeped in at Ryan. 'Thanks for looking after him.'

'My pleasure.'

RAPE

'Don't move a muscle, or I'll cut it out.' David felt a knife at his throat and spit in his ear. More rancid smells and thoughts. Adrenalin rushed. A chill cut down his spine. Frozen. Fear of pain and death caused mental garbling. Abstraction. More adrenalin. Stammered breathing.

'You're going to keep quiet. Do you hear?'

The stinking hand and fingers peeled from David's lips. Should he shout, or fight, or shit, or cry? Thoughts linked, rapid and disjointed.

'Good boy,' said the man. David's mind was in his throat as he tried to swallow. Then it was in his ears as he focused on sound. A filthy hand worked on his fly. Stinking air sat around his head. In his ear came moist sounds. Those that the mouth speaks when you're making love. Sticky, breathy, tender sounds, whispered of violence.

Keep quiet, was the only structured thought David could muster.

'Good,' said the man, reassuring and threatening. Then the knife was at David's balls, seemingly before it had left his neck. Maybe time was going backwards now and soon he'd be in the restaurant. 'Now you're going to make this real easy for me, aren't you?' The man pulled at David's jeans. 'Show me your cunt Aidsy queer. That's right. Sweet! Yeah. Sweet.'

David listened but was deaf. All he could hear was 'AIDS' repeating in his head. 'Do you know what I'm going to do to you?' David felt pain in his balls. 'Do you?' David's mind was numb. He had no thoughts. Then he had some, then nothing. AIDS was no longer a word only, it was a smell, a taste, a nauseating excitement.

'I can't hear you boy.'

No, no, no, are the words he felt. The dirty mouth produced ugly spit. Slimy and putrid, it burned a channel down the crack of David's arse.

'If you don't make this real easy for mc, I'm going to open you up with my blade. Do you understand?' The disgusting mouth spoke with a sharp bloody tongue. It severed seconds, explaining too much. 'Do you understand?'

David couldn't think, but he said, 'Yes.' An excruciating pain shot within.

Fucking bastard. Looking at me in my mirror. Flirting. I knew what you were doing, what you were saying. You're making my dick hard. Queer. Making me hard. Lovely hair. Faggot. Pussy arse. I'll show you what's what, who's the man. Making me hard. Fucking taking the piss. I'll come up your cunt. Aidsy queer. I'll cum right up your pussy. Yeah, I'm cumming. I'm cumming. Yeah. Lovely fucking arse. Lovely. Lovely. Lovely.'

David was knocked to the floor. His head became pulp. But the attacker's mind was in full speed, excited, furious, gorging, fueled.

'Making me want to fuck your cunt. Pretty girl. That's what you are. Pretty, pretty, girl. In my cab, making me hard like that. That's right. That's what you did. I knew where you lived, what your game was. I knew what you wanted. And I gave it to you. Just like you wanted.'

The cabby kicked the arse that he had just fucked. Amazed. Thrilled. His release was intense. What strength. What power. What control. A lifeless puppy lay on the floor at his disposal. Whatever he wanted to do, he could.

'You're all soft now. What time is it? Time to stick your watch up your cunt. So, you think you're clever, yeah. Stuck up bastard. Pretty, pretty fuck-head.'

'Can you tell what time it is boy?' said the cabby. This was the last thing David heard. Apart from the internal noises the body makes as it's crushed. For the next forty minutes, David was a deposit for frustration and anger.

INSIDE AND OUTSIDE

And so, I lived some more life. First seconds, then another few, then weeks and months. Remembering.

Looking out of the window I get a rush of good feelings. For all its constant moving, the city has never looked quite so still. It's evening. For some reason, there are fireworks in the sky, soundless, not awe-inspiring, but pretty, all the same. The edge of the window takes up a third of my view, putting my wall and me in the whole scene. It's easy to feel separate, detached, a part of nothing. Catching myself scowling, I cut off.

Red car, white car, red car, black cab, Rob's car. I think, no, yes it is. He's been positive twelve years now. All but one of his close friends have died. It's different for me. I'm lucky, I guess. My status doesn't really bother me. Maybe I'm not sick enough. I hope to live until I'm old.

My God, he looks sexy. I go to knock on the window, but stop. My breath steams my view. Rob becomes lumps of colour as he moves across the road and out of sight underneath me.

Sometimes I pretend it didn't happen. I never got attacked. Or, it didn't affect me much. Or, I've dealt with it and moved on. I can't remember what he smelt like, hardly anything about it. I was out cold I think, for most of it, anyway. I don't know.

The key in the door, the squeak, and his shuffling coat, all tell me Rob's home.

'Hello,' he says.

'Hello, yourself.' We are so formal. It sometimes makes us laugh, always makes us smile. And still, just getting a response from him, knowing it's for me and being sure that there is no one else he would rather it be for, makes me feel stuff, nice stuff.

'Good to have you home.'

'Oh.'

'Oh. That's clever. No, no, no, I didn't mean it.' All I want to do is hold him and so I do. Because I can, and he loves me doing it.

'Let me get my jacket off.'

'No.'

I trap his arms in his sleeves as he tries to slide it off. 'I warned you. Now. Do as I say.'

'Okay, Okay, just don't hurt me. I'm very fragile.'

'Yeah, like a rugby player.'

Rob wiggles out of his jacket and I let him go.

'What were you doing?' he says.

'Nothing.' He stretches his arms so high that his stomach shows. I love that part of him. 'I was just thinking.'

'What about?'

'Stuff.'

'What stuff?'

'Joe stuff.'

Rob looks down, shrugs and sighs. 'Do you want anything to eat?'

'What are you having?'

'Food,' he says, acting Neanderthal.

He heads towards the kitchen. My voice follows him. 'Are any of those biscuits left?'

'Maybe.' I can hear the crackling of a biscuit wrapper. 'Maybe not.'

I run into the kitchen and grab hold of Rob. 'There better be.'

Rob puts his arms around my shoulders. 'Are we still on for tonight?' he says. His lips are so close to my ear, I can feel the words. Either his breath, or the content of the question causes a sensation inside. Possibly fear and excitement mixed.

'Too right, we're on.'

'Got everything?'

'Yeah.'

'I'm going to have a bath, and relax for a while.'

'Great, I've got a couple of calls to make. What do you want to eat?'

'Whatever you're having.'

'Just a sandwich. I can't be bothered with much else.'

'Okay, that'll do nicely. I'll have it served in my bath.'

'You want it wet?'

'You're the one who's wet.'
'Blah, blah, blah, blah, blah.'

'Can you hear sheep?' says Rob and heads towards the bathroom. I put on some music and make some sandwiches. I potter around, doing nothing much, until I realise I'm avoiding making the calls. One is insignificant, a massage appointment. The other, which I've put off for weeks, is to Flora. We do manage to speak now and then. But, there's no getting away from it, our conversations are always weird, strained, only part-honest.

LOVE

Finally home, Flora took off her coat and jacket. She undressed out of her crisp, tailored smartness, simultaneously pulling on something comfortable. She flicked the switch on the kettle and reached for the television remote. Fighting and blood - the six o'clock news. She muted the sound but left the picture on. As she turned towards the kitchen she caught herself in the mirror. At first she looked away, but then looked back. Walking over to the mirror she stopped. She was curious about the face that she wore. With a voice in her head, she asked about it. Finally becoming full, busy with her own thoughts. She headed towards her computer. Fingers hovered inches above the keyboard. An idea came, then left. There were long periods of nothing, followed by involuted thoughts and puzzles. Then letters stammered from her. Words worked wrongly.

I worked so hard at our relationship, it looked easy to you, seemed natural. It wasn't. Love doesn't just happen. It's got to be worked at, molded.

Flora rubbed her hair and put her hands under her chin. The front door buzzer didn't sound, so she didn't answer it. No one headed up to her apartment. A pang of hunger distracted her from blocking out her aloneness. Leaving the computer on and the file open, Flora drifted aimlessly towards the kitchen. She poured some cereal, but finding there was no milk, she picked up the telephone and ordered some Chinese food. The numbers of the dishes came easy to her memory. As did trying to communicate the details.

'Hello, I'd like to order some food. Please, a delivery. Yes. Meal twenty-eight please, with rice. Yes. No, no sauce. That's right. Extra soy please. Yes, I know. A Coke, thanks.' The seven o'clock news came on the television. Silently and safely it showed ugly scenes. It attracted Flora's gaze. 'Yes I know. That's fine. Yes, extra please.' Holding the receiver between her shoulder and face, Flora scratched at her psoriasis. She squinted, trying to focus her eyes. The television continued to mimic events. 'For one, that's right. F.L.O.R.A. Yes, thank you. Of course.' Flora is asked to hold whilst her credit card is confirmed. David appeared on the screen. He fell into a woman's lap. How perfect,- the filming, the art direction, the styling and David. Flora's memory must have changed him, he didn't look the same. He was here in their room looking at her, but with no anger, or upset, or confusion. A tearing sensation forced its way up her torso. She threw the telephone towards the television. It cracked loudly against the screen but didn't break. David didn't wince, he was beyond her touch. Flora felt her powerlessness.

'Misses Flora. Hello, Misses Flora are you there?'

Flora was there, she knelt with her fist twisting into her gut. She lifted her head. Her eyes were wet, shut tight. Her face was crushed into an expression. Crying was painful, it meant letting go. She found this difficult.

'Misses Flora! Misses Flora! Misses Flora!'

The voice from the phone split into her head and she shrieked like she never had before.

'What!' The shock wave of this might have knocked down chairs, the table, all movable objects in the room, but it didn't.

There was silence from the telephone receiver, then a click as the other person hung-up. David was gone also. Flora was alone. She caught a glimpse of the next ad. A dog ate food from a bowl then transformed into a prince. Physically she folded into herself, then further into her memory, then beyond. The phone started to make a loud sound, to remind her it was off the hook. She got up and replaced the receiver. Instantly, it rang. She picked it up. Quickly, her voice, facial expressions, and even body posture changed.

'I don't need to know you're name,' she said. 'Just that you surrender yourself to me completely.'

'I hope it's okay to call,' said the man. 'I was given your number by George Whitehall.'

'That's okay. I hope you're as good as George. He's one of my favourites. You realise you'll have to trust me. I'm the M aster. Understand?' Flora smiled, comfortable with this control. She hears more apologetic, subservient, politeness. 'Eight o'clock. Meet me there. Good.' Flora hangs up and laughs out loud.

THERMOS

Noises. Relentless layers of sound. The shifting of bodies, breathing men, rustles, cracks, coughs and whispers. Sex could be heard. Bathhouse sex, most kinds that men do to each other. Here were old, golden and tired sounds, familiar and not unpleasant. This was constant, how could anyone feel alone.

In his cubicle, with the door ajar, Joe was absorbed, contained. His memories could be soothed here, turned to murmurings, at times silenced. He didn't need any of these men. No complications or attachments. Words weren't needed. Company was all he sought, not connection.

There were billions of ideas inside each full but hungry room. Everyone was guarded here. Sound-proofed from the haunting whole world, that can drive you to hate, or sadness. It was all still out there.

He breathed cautiously in and out, trying to find the rhythm of the others here: the get up, eat, shit, cum, go to bed, daily rhythm. The events that differentiate moments one from the other. Stubborn memories took Joe away.

'Hi Joe.'
'Ricki!'
'Are you busy?'
'No.'

Freckle-faced, with golden-Labrador-puppy hair, Ricki rolled around the door frame and pulled up one foot behind him .

'Can I come in.'
'Of course.'

Ricki sat up against the wooden wall, his towel shifting but not opening. Feeling self-conscious Joe asked. 'Are you okay?' Ricki scrutinized Joe's face. First his nose, then his cheeks, his forehead and his chin. Joe wanted to look away, but didn't. It was as though Ricki were asking questions with his eyes. As Joe watched him, he began to see, not features, but feelings and thoughts. He scuffed Ricki's head and let his hand stay on his shoulder. There was a jerking movement in Ricki's towel. Registering this, something began in Joe. Still looking, reading and trying to understand, they kissed. It was a celebration, desperate and needed.

'Looking for a three-way?' said a stranger. He had been watching from the doorway, arms folded, with a cigarette perched at the tips of his fingers. When sensing their answer, 'Don't let me stop you,' was his leaving remark.

Joe closed the door. Alone, looking and seeing all, the boy, the growing, and the perfect man. Still feeling the kiss, wanting another, then acting on this. Once again, a thud in his gut and a high in his head. Sharing each other their rhythm began. An internal pulse beat and continued.

TOGETHER

David couldn't move a muscle, he was out cold. The smell of cigarettes and alcohol permeated the room. His body was being moved around, pushed and pulled. He was being watched, lying on the floor. Naked and helpless. Pathetic, without response. David's mouth was opened and fingers pushed inside, feeling the hot wetness within. It was usually a private place, unavailable to others. But now, it was exposed, used, open for play. A dick, hard, with precum shining on the end, rubbed across the lips. Making them look greasy, lubing the way for easy access. The dick followed the outline, then moved off across David's cheek. It nestled for a moment, in the socket of one eye. The lid lifted from the pressure and the white of David's eye could be seen. The iris had rotated upwards, as though he was watching his brain, his thoughts, looking for an answer.

Both of David's lids were held open. The man doing this laughed. Finding this intriguing, he tried to fit the head of his dick under the lid. It wouldn't go. This idea was forgotten as the man moved on to other things. The pits of David's arm smelled wholesome. Enjoying this, the man lay with his face fully covered. As though suckling, he breathed in deep. Licking the pits might wash away some of the smell, so he just nuzzled and continued to take in David.

Stopping again the man watched the body. He could see smooth skin on the chest, stomach muscles and David's crotch. He decided to open David's legs, so he could see the crack of his arse and the blond hair of his inner thighs. This area was so sacred, so pure, so neglected and desired. It was a gift, to have his face here. With softness either side. He pulled David's legs together, trapping his head in between. Perfect security. Ideal sexual stimulation. The man managed to maneuver in close to David's balls, so they rested on his face. Tender and musty, they rocked in response to snuggling and kissing.

When finished, not necessarily satiated, the man knelt

and lifted David's legs up on his shoulders. He hooked them over his own, so that he could push his dick against David's arse, if he wanted to. Then, lifting further, he bent David double and gorged on his arse, licking and sticking his tongue so far in it hurt his mouth. This lasted a good ten minutes. The man jerked his own dick and would have climbed inside David's arse, if he could. Getting more inside, was exactly what he wanted to do, intended to do. But, this treat was being savored. Holding back. Wanting to extract everything, before he moved on. It wasn't that he got bored with David's arse, but he was eager to feel it. In went his finger, lubed with his own cum. Hot and precious. The inside of someone. What could be more intimate, more intrusive and commanding. Soon two fingers were in the hole, then into the man's mouth. Then into David's mouth, so he could taste his own arse, give hot saliva to lube it. Three fingers were in, then four, right up to the join of the thumb. Susceptible and welcoming, the warmth seem to massage the hand. Painfully excited, the man licked David's balls, around their base and up the fine rat tail to his stomach.

It had gone on too long. The man knew it was time to stick in his dick. No protection. No having to care if it hurt. Nothing but pleasure. Nothing held back. Intensity beyond belief. Desire beyond control. And he's fucking, and fucking, and fucking. Sweating and fucking. Clearing his dick right out of the opening, then pounding all the way in. Compulsive, assertive, and important. Committed, affecting, and special. And he cums into David with all his might. And with all his love. Intent on filling the hole, the vessel, the beautiful, most beautiful thing. When finished, the man lay spent of lust. Done with, David was left alone.

'Let me get you a coffee,' said Rob.

David had slept soundly, a Rohypnol sleep. 'I feel so groggy.'

'How many did you take?'

'Three.'

'That's a lot for you. I only ever take three, and I'm an old hand.'

'I just wanted to be really gone.'

'That you were.' Rob smirked in a saucy way. His expression explained a lot of what happened the night before. 'I let you sleep in. I've been up hours.'

'What have you been doing.'

'I've been out.' Rob got off the bed and left the room momentarily. 'I got you this,' he said returning with an unusual cactus.

'Oh. That's...beautiful?'

'No, you are.' They started to kiss. Rob put his hand under the covers and cupped David's arse. 'How is it?'

'It's alright. Not too damaged.'

'You were very relaxed.'

'I should hope so. What happened?'

'That's my business. But you can imagine.'

David's dick got hard. 'Yeah, I can.'

RESOLUTION

Knightsbridge, Hyde Park, Green Park, -the Piccadilly line heading towards the West End. David watched as people avoided watching him. He closed his eyes and felt very close to tears. There was no particular reason for this. It was familiar, almost boring to him. Unhappiness? Nothing felt that clear. Something wasn't right, unless this was how people were meant to feel. This is how he accepted it. David assumed everyone carried near surfacing emotions around with them all the time. But, he thought, some were more sensitive to their feelings than others. Having come from the Chelsea and Westminster Hospital David was full of disease. Hospitals, especially HIV centers, always had this effect on him. When leaving his doctor, he usually felt as though his virus,-getting the attention it desired, was content that it filled his body, his mind and his soul.

A woman beside David was reading *Cosmopolitan,* an article about sex and food. David skimmed over it. If only things were so black and white, so uncomplicated. He yawned. Over in the window his reflection looked as disjointed as it always did. Seeing himself made him think about his age. He looked down at what he was wearing and saw his hands, this comforted him, they were familiar.

The tube stopped at Piccadilly. David was going to get out at Covent Garden. Some people got off. Others got on. A strong smell of apples came on with someone. It was artificial, not like sweets, more soapy. There was a huge man with a sweaty forehead. No, it didn't seem likely that it was him. A red-haired woman with an Asian looking baby, possibly. David moved his attention onto an old chalky-skinned black woman. She wore red football socks that pulled up over the knee and a Macdonald's paper jacket. David heard some commotion to his left. Someone had just missed the door closing but had caught their bag. David saw it being tugged free, then turned to see who was at the other end of it. At the same time the other person turned and caught David's eye. It was Joe.

David had seen pictures of Joe now and then in *Time Out*

and a couple of the fashion magazines. When he saw these photos, he'd invariably stare at them and keep the magazine around longer than he normally would.

Joe moved behind David, the window separating them. Smells and people muffled, colours muted. Although Joe was behind two layers of dirty glass he seemed so much more tangible. Simply, these two looked at each other and communicated. Joe began to write on the window. David couldn't make sense of it, he was only half concentrating, still looking, wanting and trying to see beyond all he knew. The train jerked. Joe's finger slipped but managed to finish what he was writing. Still David didn't read it because Joe was holding up his fist, he was opening two of his fingers and his thumb and facing this towards David. As the train moved off Joe's hand followed slightly, his facial expression was sure and as determined as he could make it. What David didn't see was how this deteriorated as the train left the station. Joe dropped his hand and "I love you" became a fist.

David's focus was beyond the window seeing Joe sliding out of sight. Only when he was in the tunnel did he read the writing. Joe had written it so it could be read the right way round for David. It said, "trust me." The "s" was back to front and the "m" had a jagged line through it where the train had jolted, but it was clear enough. So clear that at that moment it cut through everything. It were as though everything finally made sense. Flora flashed into David's mind, so many events and reconstruction of meaning. Pictures in his head changed. Memories swapped. Feelings grew in different directions. The last five years seemed to re-allocate all it's content. David turned to see sniggers and whispers from some school girls. The man with the sweaty head was blushing. This made David do the same. The woman and baby were replaced by a teenage boy who sneered aggressively. David looked away, trying to sort through his mind. His eyes fell on the old woman with the football socks. She chewed slowly on a toffee and watched him. David looked away, but the sound of sucking teeth brought his attention back to her. Slowly she nodded her head down, up, and back so far that it seemed she caught it just before it toppled off. Her neck was etched with white lines of dry skin. Now she was smiling too, a flat-old-didn't-have-much-energy-but-wanted-everything-for - David smile. Old and tied, she closed her eyes. Without opening her mouth she said' 'Mm hmm,' which turned into a cough. David knew what he had to do.

Back at Piccadilly station, Joe stood alone. A crowed quickly refilled the platform. They jostled, no one seemed to care what had happened. Joe felt very other, -sexually, completely. The next train arrived within minutes, soon enough for Joe to still be within the same thoughts. Getting on and standing by the door, still nothing outside registered. The train set off, rattled, then stopped again, still nothingness. The doors opened at Leicester Square and a hand reached in. It took hold of Joe's arm.

'Joe.'

Coming out of his dream, then moving into a better one Joe saw David standing on the platform.

'You waited for me.'

'Yeah, I did.'

'What, why?'

'Because I trust you, stupid.'

Joe stepped off the train. They both stood motionless. Then as though pushed from behind they fell into each other and held tight. Nothing had ever felt so comfortable, nothing for either of them. This is how they stayed for a while. The train left. People watched. David and Joe were in their own world, beyond all the hatred and cruelty that could ever be imagined. No one could touch them now. This was strong and believed and fine. They pulled apart, but kept hold of each others arms.

'You know that whatever you were told isn't true don't you.' There was so much pleading in Joe's voice, too much hurt.

'I do now.' Again they held each other. A wolf-whistle came from somewhere behind them and they could only laugh.

Half smiling, but with tears in his eyes Joe asked. 'Are you seeing anyone?'

'Yeah, for three years now.' This didn't deter Joe, somehow he knew better.

'Are you in love?'

'Yeah I am.'

'Oh.' Before Joe could realise his response David continued.

'With you.'

'But, what about...' Joe's words were stopped by David's hand.

'It's fine. I think he already knows.'

Also available

The Cruelty of Silence

Sebastian Beaumont

The Cruelty of Silence is the highly anticipated new novel from the author of *On the Edge, Heroes Are Hard to Find* and *Two*. This subtle and intensely atmospheric novel begins on the anniversary of the enigmatic disappearance of successful architect Alex Stern. His lover, Lol, has to spend a deeply distracted year looking for him – at the cost of both his job and of the comfortable home they shared. After much frustration and an inability to restart his life, Lol discovers that a large sum of money is missing and that a locked computer file may contain the vital clue to what really happened to Alex. Set in Edinburgh, Spain, Paris and Amsterdam, *The Cruelty of Silence* is a taut and compelling contemporary mystery. It is also a striking account of the rewards and tensions of family life, the confusion created by new love, of pop music and drugs . . .

ISBN 1-873741-30-8

£9.50

Thresholds

David Patrick Beavers

Set in early summer 1977, *Thresholds* is at once a claustrophobic and intensely sensual novel about three eighteen year olds idling away time as they decide what to do with their lives. Brian has been left Kehmeny Court, a house with rambling grounds, on the Pacific coast near San Francisco. Living with him are his fiancée Viola and his best friend Morgan. Everything should be idyllic – but discontent is about to bring change. Brian is falling out of love with Viola and, perhaps, in love with Morgan. Meanwhile Morgan, who has been in love with Brian since childhood, finds love now becomes sexual. David Patrick Beavers – author of *Jackal in the Dark* and *The Jackal Awakens* – focuses on the erotic turmoil that seems so much a part of late adolescence to produce a novel that is nostalgic, powerful and stimulating.

ISBN 1-873741-28-6

£8.50

Oddfellows

Jack Dickson

Oddfellows marks an auspicious debut for Scottish novelist Jack Dickson. This is the story of Joe Macdonald, dishonourably discharged from the army, who becomes a bouncer for – and lover to – nightclub owner and entrepreneur Billy King. Their relationship is all about power – Billy commands, Joe obeys. But when Joe intervenes after Billy commits a particularly brutal rape of a fourteen year old, things become more uncomfortable. And not just for Joe. Drawn into this web of double dealing, violence and murder are Joe's teenage nephew Sean and appealing policeman Andy Hunter. Located in Glasgow's gay and criminal underworlds and encompassing child abuse, drugs and sado-masochism, *Oddfellows* is a starkly delineated novel about aspects of gay life that many would rather ignore.

ISBN 1-873741-29-4

£9.99

Brutal

Aiden Shaw

Now in its third edition, *Brutal* is a raw and powerful debut novel which explores the life of a young man who makes a living as a prostitute. Paul, with the help of therapy, is trying to challenge what he has become – a person out of control on drugs and alcohol, desiring abusive and degrading sex, estranged from people he once loved. Moreover, he is facing his own mortality while living with H.I.V. Increasingly disappointed by the way men relate to each other, he discovers that there are women around him to whom he cam turn.

Set mainly in London's underground club scene – where drug use is commonplace and casual sex something of an inevitability -*Brutal* offers an extraordinary, sometimes bleak portrait of a lost generation for whom death is as much a companion as lovers, friends, and family. Yet this is far from being a dispirited novel, and although the subject matter may shock, the shining honesty of the writing will prove life-affirming and an inspiration.

ISBN 1-873741-24-3

£8.50

The Learning of Paul O'Neill

Graeme Woolaston

The Learning of Paul O'Neill follows the eponymous hero over nearly thirty years – from adolescence in Scotland in the mid-sixties to life in a South Coast seaside resort in the seventies and eighties and a return to a vibrant Glasgow in the early nineties. As the novel begins, fifteen year old Paul is learning fast about sexuality as his Scottish village childhood disintegrates around him. After many years in England, he returns to Scotland trying to come to terms with the sudden death of his lover and to establish himself as a writer. His return brings him face to face with the continuing effects of adolescent experiences he thought he had put behind him – some enriching, some of which have directly informed his sexual nature. And the influence of an ambiguous, handsome, married bisexual man raises new questions about the shape of Paul's life as he arrives at the threshold of middle-age. *The Learning of Paul O'Neill* is a compelling and adult novel about gay experience and aspects of sexuality which some may find shocking but which are written about with an honesty that is as refreshing as it is frank.

ISBN 1-873741-12-X

£7.50

The Biker Below the Downs

Graeme Woolaston

Another thought-provoking novel about aspects of gay life not usually explored in fiction. When John – a middle-aged and well heeled Scot on holiday in a small Sussex village – first sees his leather-clad biker neighbour he feels an immediate attraction. And both are aware of it. After an encounter with a naked youth in the neighbour's garden, John realises the two boys are lovers and that he is attracted to both. But a chance remark made by the biker leads John to make a set of discoveries which shock and move him. The story of a man discovering the son he didn't know he had and a boy discovering the father he'd never known, *The Biker Below the Downs* is compelling, richly comic and strongly erotic.

ISBN 1-873741-25-1

£8.50